Charles Russell Christian

The Mountain Bard

A Series of Original Poems

Charles Russell Christian

The Mountain Bard
A Series of Original Poems

ISBN/EAN: 9783337289652

Printed in Europe, USA, Canada, Australia, Japan

Cover: Foto ©Andreas Hilbeck / pixelio.de

More available books at **www.hansebooks.com**

THE

Mountain Bard;

A SERIES OF ORIGINAL POEMS.

BY C. RUSSELL CHRISTIAN.

ENLARGED EDITION.

HUNTINGTON, W. VA.
PRINTED AT THE ARGUS BOOK AND JOB OFFICE.
1885.

THE DEDICATION.

———:o:———

HUNTINGTON, January 2, 1885.

DEAR SIR—

In republishing these pieces how shall I address myself to the public? Like one of England's Bards, I hardly know whether to regard myself as building a monument or as bury- ing the dead. I have been for six years the pioneer of Song in this songless land; and when I would have laid down my pen in disgust, and retired from the dangerous paths of Song, it was at your request that I again entered the field, and with the motto of "Try, try again," took up anew the burden of Life.

As to how I have succeeded, the world may judge for itself. But those whose friendship I most desire, and to re- ceive whose approval is my highest ambition, will not be led by unfair criticism to doubt my honest endeavor to sow the seeds of literature in this hitherto barren land.

To you these rhymes are justly due for encouragements extended when Hope itself had begun to fail.

C. RUSSELL CHRISTIAN.

To DR. W. P. BRYAN.

ERRATA.

In the following table only those errors are noted which might obscure the sense intended. Also some changes recommended by the author:

Page 16, line 14, read " signs " for " sign."

Page 26, line 2. read "in ruins overcast."

Page 31, line 2₁, read "ravishment " for " vanishment."

Page 41, line 1, include " a " in quotation.

Pages 50 and 51, let final line of each stanza of " The Deity" be " Alas for human love below !"

Page 76, line 5, read " 'Tis " for " Tie."

Page 98. line 21, read " solace " for " salace."

Page 102, line 3, insert " land " after " and."

Page 103, line 28, read " setst " for " sets."

Page 104, line 8, read "charge " for " feat."

Page 118, line 6, read " Americ's " for " Amric's."

TABLE OF CONTENTS.

————:o:————

PART FOURTH.

PART FIFTH.

PART SIXTH.

PART SEVENTH.

THE

Mountain Bard.

PART FIRST.

THE SONG OF WAR.

OF War to overturn a thousand thrones—
   War to establish Barbarism and Night—
Loud War to drown a thousand victims' groans,
   Sing—fiery Muse!—and guide the strains aright!
The voice of War—to say the least—is doom ;
   The tread of War is ruin to the land ;
The crown of War is Death's most horrid plume ;
   The rights of War are written in the sand.
War roars—and horrid thunder shakes the spheres !
   War sleeps—and Peace attempts to heal the wound ;
War speaks—and vengeance of a thousand years
   Urges the fray, and scatters bale around :—
Thus hath it been—shall be – since War began,
   Foe to the world—to Science—and to man !

The Foot-Prints of Time.

FULL many a ruined tower is rescued from beneath the
        sands,
Wrought o'er with pictured-language by the long-forgotten
        bands ;
Thus many an ancient record leaps into the living light,
And Day advances slowly—slowly—toward the seat of Night;
And many an ancient monarch, though his latest resting-
        place,
No more can boast the column reared in honor of his race,
And though his name be blotted from the records of the Past,
Still lives in his examples—lives, and lives until the last !
The touch of Death is ruin to this tenement of clay ;
Man dies—but his examples live until the latest day !
The touch of Death is fatal to the mortal overwrought ;
Man dies—but his examples live and mold a world of thought!
A vasty wheel is set in motion at the early morn,
Too soon the motor falls asleep, and from the scene is borne ;
And yet around its axle, rolling onward in its might,
The wheel with its momentum whirls—and whirls until the
        night !   .
A voice from out the ruins of the ages long ago
Cries out, " The dead survive the death—the future age shall
        show !"
The shallow-hearted gentry of the present ages, drink
From many a living fount—why not ?—yet never pause to
        think
That where they sit in pleasure with the beings they adore,
Their fathers shook the bloody lance, and braved the battle's
        roar !
The pools are filled with water now that once were filled with
        blood ;
And ripest fruits are shaking where the ranked warriors
        stood ;
The sword is now a plowshare, and the spear a pruning hook ;
The voice of Truth around the hearth, of Love beside the
        brook ;

The wells are filled with water, and the ci'y's walls are high,
And e'en the voice of Death is smooth—his reign is passing
    by—
But oh! the voice historic speaks, and fills the world with
    gloom;
The Past is but an oracle to teach the coming doom!
The temple-dome of Freedom, reared aloft, amid the tears
Of many thousand thousands, is the produce of the years;
The gazing wall—the only refuge from the godless horde—
Was reared aloft, one hand at work—the other on the sword;
Thus ages, till at last one land re-echoes Freedom's tread—
But every pillar of the State is pillowed on the dead!
The myriad ages, rolling onward through the boundless Past,
Bequeathed to one another all their burden as they passed,
Until the mighty whirlwind, heaving onward in its course,
Collided with the present—losing nothing of its force—
Then on again the Causes through the Future as the Past,
Producing grand effect which lives—and lives until the last!
The rise and fall of systems by the thousand come and go,
And scarce a living trace remains to scorn the overthrow;
A darkness born of Death is rolling onward from the East;
The waves of Lethe roll where Science held a royal feast!
The gleam of light that still remains is pushing toward the
    West—
The star of Freedom, like the Sun, cannot afford to rest;
The war—the peace—the good—the crime—the ignorance—
    the wit—
Raise man at times to Paradise, then drag him to the Pit;
The while his great examples stand—and stand until the
    last—
And present ages prosper on the ruins of the Past.

THE GLANCE AT WAR.

I.

THE roar of guns—the clash of swords and spears—
Shall be my song—my Muses, blood and tears!
Vainly may Man expect the hills to bloom
With aught but flowers to deck his early tomb,
While warriors hold their stainless names and free;
While o'er the frightened waste of land and sea
The infernal War-cloud rolls in fierce disdain,
Darker than Night and pillowed on the slain!

II.

Ages of Peace contribute to refine
Untutored Man that bends before her shrine;
While Science in profusion pours the light
Scorning Disaster and repelling Night—
And o'er the Earth subjected to her sway
Unfurls the standard and the powers of Day.
'T is now the murderer meets with justice due;
'T is now the thief finds other work to do;
'T is now that Perjury—covered with disgrace—
Withdraws from Man and hides his withering face;
Adultery now must curb her far delight;
Now Arson ceases to disturb the night;
And blood-stained Villainy from his ancient throne
Falls in dishonor—powerless and alone—
While Man in triumph all the paths may trace
Of universal, undisputed Peace.

III.

Thus governs Peace; but in Oblivion far
Sink light and justice 'neath the power of War,
That with monarchic strides upturns the ground—
Throned on the flames that scatter bale around;
For Peace—though clad in more than regal state—
Expires beneath the burden when the weight

Of War oppresses that with hostile hand,
O'erthrows proud armies and o'erwhelms the land!
The warrior's trade is founded deep in strife
Where Life expires and Death aspires to life;
Where'er the warrior treads the trembling sod
He sends the myriads forth to meet their God!
Enthroned on War to scourge the guilty land,
With shining spears upheld in either hand,
Sublime he rides o'er fields of human gore—
Hears music in the infernal cannon's roar—
And smiles on cities wrapped in sheets of flame—
And lisps in secret, " *This will give me fame!*"
The course of War is marked by ghastly Death;
Both State and Church surrender now their breath,
And to the honored sepulcher of Fame
Resign their *vigor* and pick up their *name!*
While loud and louder sound the dread alarms—
A universal shout—" To arms! To arms!"
And soon as called, ten thousand warriors move
Their skill in slaughtering human foes to prove;
And years of tumult roll across the land,
And hideous crimes arise and take their stand.

IV.

'T is now the thief in all his fiendish power,
Infests the land—disturbs the midnight hour—
And fearless, prowling where no law survives—
Or, if surviving, writhing in the gyves—
Lays impious hands on moneys not his own,
Removes the treasure and departs unknown;
'T is now that Perjury stalks amid the land,
And swears to fight for this or t' other band.
But finds no sooner victory with his foes
Than in their scale his final weight he throws!
'T is now the murderer marks his ancient foe,
And from the silent ambush " lays him low;"
Then turns a patriot, and in Stentor tones
Praises the War and drowns his victim's groans—
And trusting in the CODE OF WAR TO SAVE,
Treads unrepentant o'er his victim's grave!
Nor stops the power of infamy with men;
The *milder sex* forsake their course amain;
Incest, Adultery and their kindred crimes
Flock round the camp and breed their kind betimes;

And when true Chastity in all her charms
Is found in woman that disdains his arms,
Some heartless villain—used to scenes of gore—
Fit school to learn crimes shuddered at before—
Breeds impious rape in his infernal brain,
Seizes—and spoils—and leaves her in disdain!

V.

'T is now the Hero waves his sword on high,
And calls aloud for "those who dare to die;"
And drives his men o'er fields of flame and smoke
Where thousands cease to breathe at every stroke!
Now flash their fiery swords aloft in air,
And twice ten thousand spears reflect the glare;
And countless steeds bewildered scour the plain,
Bestrewed with gory fragments of the slain!
The roar of guns is echoed far around
In tones at once that shake both air and ground;
The roll of drums—the clash of swords and spears—
Unseat the soul and seem to shake the spheres;
While flaps his wing Destruction o'er the plain,
And gluts himself insatiate on the slain!
As two fierce clouds—o'erfraught with power and rage—
Throned on opposing winds, in war engage
And rush together heedless of the cost,
Till—in each other swallowed up and lost—
Their bolts miscarry, while the winds wheel round
And dash them both in torrents to the ground:
So rush the warriors of the human race,
With shock to jar a nation from its place!
Weary at length of coping thus with Death,
The fight suspends—the warrior draws his breath;
And Truce—advancing—bids the tumult cease,
And countless hearts beat high in hopes of Peace;
And many a voice is tuned of warrior stained
To chant "*Te Deum*" for the battle gained!
But hark! the dread commander calls his bands,
And through the trump proclaims his dread commands:
"Advance ye braves! Let every freeman strike!
Advance gallants, with saber, gun and pike!
Our cause on record shows who 's in the right;
A glorious victory soon shall end the fight!

Behold the amazement in the opposing powers!
Stand firm amid the War-cloud as it lowers!
Some o our hearts will doubtless cease to beat
Ere the opposing legions call retreat;
Yet be it so! His be the noblest bed
Who sinks entombed the deepest 'mid the dead!
With zeal renewed now charge the fiendish foe;
Shout ' Victory!' Now let the bugle blow!
Wave high your arms with all your valiant might!
The charge! The charge! Renew the dreadful fight!"
Meanwhile on t' other side—with equal noise—
Commanders urge the fray amid the pause;
Then all stand waiting for the dread alarms,
Til! martial music sounds the shock of arms!
Then loudly swells the wild, tumultuous roar,
In tones unheard around that dell before:
The seated hills are trembling with the sound;
Infernal thunders fling their bolts around;
And belching engines fill with living flame
The glen from which the warrior plucks his fame!

VI.

O righteous Heaven! arm—arm Thy power to save,
When Man thus trembles o'er one common grave!
No arm but Thine can bring the timely aid
While lives a brave to flash the gleaming blade;
O righteous Heaven! bid storms of tumult cease,
And plant instead Thy sacred banner Peace!
'T is Thine in war or peace--'t 's Thine alone—
To scorn Man's power and to assert Thine own;
Then deign for once to plant Thy foot sublime
On War's dread engines and erase the crime!

VII.

As, when the Storm-wind bids the ocean roar,
The frightened seaman—drifting toward the shore—
Exerts his utmost skill but all in vain,
And sinks entombed deep in the watery main:
E'en so the sons of Peace—oppressed by War—
Refuse the sword and seeking climes afar,
In distant lands meet tragic death alone,
Or fall at home—unhonored and unknown!
Enthroned on War, where'er the legions roll,
They bring both land and sea to their control;

O'erthrow proud States regardless of their worth ;
Drive science—morals—virtue from the earth—
And with demeanor grim—ferocious—fell—
Hurl myriads trembling headlong down to Hell !
Nor is this fiendish game of modern birth ;
'T is ancient almost as the trodden earth !
What Cain began—through zeal or malice wrought—
Mankind have followed up, and thus have brought
Destruction—pillage—slaughter—tears and gore—
To every age—and frightened every shore !
And thousands—are they shattered by the moon ?
Desire no higher inscription—kinglier boon—
Than warlike titles on their worthless names—
The signs of pillage, slaughter, tears and flames !

VIII.

To War 't is given to rule both Church and State,
And dub her heroes with the title " Great;"
But whence their greatness came 't were hard to tell ;
For no true greatness can in Hero dwell
Who wins his way with sword and spear to fame,
In hopes to shed some lustre on his name,
Unless it were his great desire to fight—
The greatness boasted by the Prince of Night !
Yet, strange to say, since first the world began,
Mankind—at constant enmity with *Man*—
Have in pursuit of *greatness* levied wars,
And plucked its honored trophies—blood and scars—
With all the dignity to mortals known,
And gloried in their hearts of hardened stone !
War is a vice that since the world began,
Hath dwelt enshrined within the heart of Man
In both his savage state and *civilized*,
And as some priceless jewel hath been prized !
O, shame to men who wear the title " Great,"
That War hath been the plague of every State !
The Babylonian Empire rose on War ;
The Persian marched behind its flaming car ;
Judea rose to power with trump and sword !
And Egypt, Syria, Greece and Rome afford
Examples more of what that game hath done
That fixes Millions in the power of One.

And where are all those ancient nations now?
When took their rise and fall?—and why?—and how?—
Go ask of War—the arbitress of Fate,
The ancient mistress of both Church and State—
'T is there a record long and dread is found,
Of all the miseries Time has brought around:
Of death by famine—pestilence—the spear—
Fire—water—hope and sorrow—all save *fear!*
What then is War? A curse the direst known—
The game for fools—the wheel of Satan's throne!

IX.

And when 't is o'er, and Peace returned to life,
Bids tumult cease and every form of strife,
Who wears renown? Whose name is praised in song?
Who wears the crown by princes worn so long?
Ask CÆSAR who usurped the power in Rome,
When Pompey slumbered in his narrow home!
Ask CROMWELL who dethroned the Norman race,
And whom he chose to fill their ancient place!
If these refuse to tell the crimes they've done,
Demand of France her First Napoleon;
And if he fail the world may rise instead
And answer through the millions of her dead!
H   cease we then; let us survey no more
T   hoary registers of War and Gore;
If   e pause we, glancing into future time
B   nd the death of Misery and of Crime—
I   il the time when War's alarms shall cease,
F   ail the dawning of eternal Peace!

————:o:————

AN OATH ON A SWORD.

————

OOK at the Sword—it once was deemed a god!
   And even Peace its fabled virtues sung;
The mailed knights in ranked phalanx stood,
   And touched the blade, on gleaming hilt uphung,
And spoke the truth—spoke in the name of Sword!
   Such was the god that Chivalry adored!

To an Old Sword.

THY ancient fame is overcast ;
  And thou art falling far and fast
Toward dark Oblivion of the Past,
          O bloody Sword !

Shame to the cause that gave thee fame—
To thee, a tyrant yet, the same
As when began the tyrant's game,
          O bloody Sword !

Thou wert a god in days of yore,
By whom the knights of Chivalry swore,
For whom gallants their honors bore,
          O bloody Sword !

Yea, blazing pomp adorned thy blade ;
And none could tell thou shouldst be made
A scorn—o'erthrown—reviled—betrayed,
      O bloody Sword !

But thou art proved to be—in sooth—
A fiend that, wrapped in blood of Youth,
Strives to impede the course of Truth,
          O bloody Sword !

Down then with thee and all thy wars !
Hail to the overthrow of Mars !
Hail patriotism without thy scars,
      O bloody Sword !

THE GLANCE THROUGH TIME.

I.

STOOD to take one retrospective view
  Back through the rise and fall of mighty States;
A dreadful scene for Thought to wander through,
  Where Failure stands a-shrieking in the gates;
Place—Power—and Action in one dread immense
Lay chained to Ruin hideous and intense!

II.

There Darkness spreads her jealous wings around
  And shields from day the kingdoms of Distress;
There Superstition levels with the ground
  The spires of Lore, and boasts of her success;
And as the course of Time goes rolling by,
Destruction pilfers all beneath the sky!

III.

The gazing towers—the cities on the hills—
  And every structure built in earlier time
Fall tottering down; the wail of Misery fills
  The freighted air and terrorizes Crime;
And from the seat of carnage flies amain
The spirit of Liberty in proud disdain.

IV.

In times afar arises forth the name
  Of Babylon's monarch throned a king of terror;
And after him the Persian grasps at fame,
  And gains his victory through Belshazzar's error;
Then thundering on through ages nearer still,
Comes Alexander conquering at his will!

V.

Four mighty kingdoms next in order stand
  From Alexander's torn with sword and lance;
Four blood-stained Dynasties with crimson band
  Uphold the scepter and the power of Chance;

Then Rome from off the banks of Tiber leaps,
O'erthrows and piles the Eastern World on heaps!

VI.

The wail of Carthage tears the ancient sky,
    And calls in vain to her enraged foes;
The Romans o'er their ancient boundary fly
    And hurl the dart 'mid War's enduring throes;
Thus rolls the War till finding foes no more,
They heap with suicide their native shore!

VII.

Meanwhile Jerusalem—where the ancient Jew
    In safety dwelt and prospered age on ages—
By Heathen armies compassed round and through,
    Presents a scene that scorns historic pages;
The great theocracy of Heaven o'erthrown,
Jerusalem swims in blood but can't atone!

VIII.

Next great Mahomet breaks the massive chain
    That held Arabia to her ancient shore;
The Persian, Tartar and the Turk amain
    Cast off their gyves so long endured before;
Four evil Spirits in these kingdoms stood,
And each in turn bedrenched the earth with blood!

IX.

The summit gained at cost of useless pain,
    We now survey earth's greatest, bloodiest war;
We see heroic blood poured out as rain
    To hurl or check Napoleon's flaming car;
Then turn we from the vision in disgust,
And hide our mouth astonished in the dust!

X.

Away w th War! Through ages gone before
    Naught can be found to last but War and Death;
State, Church and Dynasty amid the roar
    Fall tottering downward and resign their breath;
While dread Disaster wraps the world with flame,
And shouts in Stentor tones the warrior's name!

XI.

O what a failure it would seem is Man,
　　Whose course we now survey from age to age!
When in derision he presumed to scorn
　　Sublimer things to vent his ceaseless rage!
His mind is flooded with Egyptian night;
He wars and dies—but sees no dawn of light!

XII.

This I beheld when I presumed to view
　　A glance through Time; I then beheld the cloud
Of dark Oblivion fringed with ether blue
　　Fall o'er the scene enwrapped as with a shroud;
The loftiest towers reached forth their peering head,
But round their base eternal darkness spread!

XIII

And as I stood and gazed upon the scene
　　Of earth in ruin thus outspread before,
I seemed as standing on the brink between
　　Life, Death and Ruin;—while amid the roar
Of Elemental war the powers of Night
Enclosed around me far—a hideous sight.

XIV.

And as I stood and viewed the Realm of Pain
　　By Night and War o'erthrown and ancient Time,
I wondered whether these dark powers would deign
　　To war with me—these powers so dread sublime—
A voice from out the ruined wrecks replied,
" *Learn wisdom now, and cast away thy pride!*"

THE VISION OF THE WORLD.

I.

I STOOD to take one retrospective view
    Back through the mighty regions of the Past ;
A dreadful scene for Thought to wander through,
    O'erspread with ruins and in darkness cast ;
Forgotten ruins of a thousand States,
Whose lost career no blazing page relates ;
Or how they stood beneath the blaze of Day,
The foes of Truth—the engines of Decay ;
How framed the friendly leagues with neighboring States,
Or proudly stood defiant in the gates :
Or this—or that—the very ruins--decayed—
Speak loudly of the warrior's fiery blade
That heaped the land—the seat of wildest crime- -
O'erthrown in tumult round the course of Time.

II.

There Desolation holds eternal sway,
Throned on the ruined pillars of Decay ;
There dread Disaster hovers o'er the plain,
The herald of Destruction's awful reign ;
And Superstition—still untaught to feel—
Borne on a thousand years of bigot zeal,
Pours o'er the scene a flood of useless tears,
And scorns the lessons of a thousand years ;
While conscious Nature—shuddering—hails her doom,
The death—the night—the chaos of the tomb !

III.

Years roll on years,—but not the flight of Time
Can hurl Disaster from the seat of crime :
Where'er the foot of man hath pressed the sod,
There hath the Tyrant swayed the Oppressor's rod ;
There hath the blood of thousand years been spilt
That Innocence might sacrifice to Guilt !

What marvel then, if o'er this seat of crime
Disaster reigns—the avenging rod of Time?
What marvel if Destruction rear aloft
Her tortured visage   never seen too oft—
And o'er the scene unwonted visions cast,
The scourge of Time—the terror of the Past?
Let nations drop the Oppressor's iron rod,
And sow the seed where former warriors trod;
Let Love assume the present throne of Hate—
And where is proud Disaster's rising State?
Till then—though Misery groans above the bier—
And Pity sheds the sympathizing tear—
While Memory lives   each vision—like the last—
Shall hail Disaster monarch of the Past!
The law of Nature—still unchanged and just—
Condemns mankind and all his works to dust,
Yet leaves this consolation still behind,
That ev'n in ruins Man may solace find—
A solace known to few, in pondering o'er
The rise and fall of what appears no more.

IV.

Shall Man forever grope his way to find
O'er ruined chaos—dark and undefined?
Shall lessons 'graved in blood upon the page
Of Time, confuse mankind from age to age?
Thus hath it been—shall be—since Time began—
Time's greatest lessons—still unknown to Man—
In dark confusion—ruin—and decay—
Have sought repose while ages rolled away!
Not that the fall of many a tyrant State
Contains no lessons for the wise and great;
The source of Truth—in far Oblivion cast—
Still springs a fountain—gleaming through the Past—
Yet holds itself aloof from Man, because
He halts before the effect—and not the cause.

V.

The records left upon the blazing page
Of sad Experience, speaks from age to age—
A voice almost prophetic—doomed at last
To reach the future ages as the past—

Speaks of the power of universal Cause,
And bids the nations heed her changeless laws.
Here then, when Man will ponder o'er the scene
Of what appears as yet, and what hath been—
When mortals deign one lingering look to cast
Back through the mighty regions of the Past—
The Present ceases,—former ages roll
Around the thinking temple of the Soul ;
What once was hidden now is doubly plain,
And Cause alone asserts eternal reign !

VI.

Away with Chance !   There never was such god,
Though feared wherever mortals press the sod ;
Whatever feat is done—a martyr burned—
A haughty warrior to his land returned—
The Tree of Knowledge robbed of half its sway,
Or mortals driven from its shades away—
No matter what—the burden straight is cast
On this fell superstition of the Past ;
Yet not the whole of Adam's race adore
This senseless Chance—this superstitious lore—
To some each ruin seems the avenging rod,
Each traitor crime the work of Mercy's God !
But who aspires to cast one look behind
To view the produce of immortal Mind—
To him no hidden hand directs the fate
That ends the sway of each tyrannic State ;
Before each ruin still he deigns to pause—
And from the effect displayed—divines the Cause.

————:o:————

WAR AND PEACE.

————

PEACE is a fabric built with labor great,
   The true foundation of both Church and State ;
War is a monster that with gory hands
Hews down the fabric and o'erwhelms the lands.

THE REIGN OF PEACE.

NOW Love may hold his universal reign
  Beside the brook—the sea—and o'er the plain ;
Now Scince steers aloft her proud career,
And gains new victories for each coming year ;
And Justice reigns in every terrene court,
And Truth—returning—hails the blest resort ;
While o'er the realm of Chaos and of Night
Eternal Progress spreads her wings of light.
And Order rises from the vast Sublime
And stamps her impress on the sands of Time.

————:o:————

THE SONG OF PEACE.

OF Peace to re-erect a thousand thrones—
  Peace to establish Intellectual Light—
Strong Peace to soothe a thousand victims' groans,
  Sing—Heavenly Muse!—and guide the strains aright!
The voice of Peace—to say the least—is love ;
  . The tread of Peace is healthful to the land ;
The crown of Peace is mercy from above ;
  The rights of Peace on endless ages stand.
Peace smiles and nations echo to the glance ;
  Peace sleeps—and War attempts to strike a blow !
Peace speaks—and Truth outshines the sword and lance,
  And threatens Ignorance with overthrow :—
Thus hath it been—shall be—since Peace began,
Friend to the world—to Science—and to man !

PART SECOND.

———◦⊰⋅⊱◦———

THE SONG OF OBLIVION.

OF dark Oblivion and the woes that dwell
    In Lethe's flood—in ruin far o'ercast—
Sing—horrid Muse!—and let the echoes swell
    In living numbers through the aged Past!
Thy voice—Oblivion!—is the voice of Woe!
    Thy empire Ruin—and thy throne the tomb!
Thy woeful echoes fill the Long Ago,
    And pour the vengeance of eternal gloom!
Thy curtain falls—and lo! 'tis horrid Night
    Where stood the blazing enginery o' Day!
The waves of Lethe breaking 'gainst the light
    O'erwhelm the Past in terror and decay:—
Thus hath it been—shall be—from pole to pole—
    Oblivion reigns—the terror of the soul!

———:0:———

OBLIVION

I.

UPON a high o'erhanging rock I stood,
    And cast a stone into the floods below me;
And as it fell, remembered that the sword
    Of Death could in an instant overthrow me!
        Ev'n as into the billows sunk the stone,
        So sink mankind into Oblivion!

II.

Before a wildly burning fire I stood,
  And cast a leaf into the flames before me;
And as it burned, remembered that the sword
  Of Death could in an instant triumph o'er me!
    Ev'n as the leaflet scorched amid the flames,
    So in Oblivion perish human names!

III.

Far from the storm's revolving wheel I stood,
  And viewed its mad career with fear and sorrow;
And as it raved, remembered that the sword
  Of Death could work for me a strange to-morrow!
    Ev'n as revolves the whirlwind through the skies,
    So dark Oblivion rolls when Nature dies!

IV.

Before a furnace redly-hot I stood,
  And cast an ore into the flames before me;
And gazing on, remembered that the sword
  Of Death could gain no greater victory o'er me!
    Ev'n as the ore survives its fiery doom,
    So man survives Oblivion and the tomb!

————:o:————

THE OBLIVION OF DEATH.

I.

I STOOD awhile to gaze upon the woe
  Wrought by the powers of dark Oblivion;
Straight it appeared as floods that overthrow
  Amid their billows the unconscious stone:
    Then I remembered the devouring sword
    Of Death whose victories I had long deplored.

II.

I gazed awhile and penned the vision down;
  Straight it appeared as when the maddening flames
Aspire to scorch a leaflet cast therein;
  Ev'n so Oblivion swallows human names!
    Again I gazed and thought upon the sword
    Of Death whose vengeance I could least afford.

III.

This vision too I gazed and thought to pen—
　When lo! Oblivion, like a cloud of woe,
On whirlwinds driven athwart the ruined plain
　Of Memory's empire, threatening overthrow!
　I gazed awhile the scene in ruins poured,
　And thought of Death—and trembled at his sword!

IV.

I saw again, but did not write in full
　To show to others;—straight the cry arose,
While swelled my heart in pity for such fool,—
　" 'Tis infidel! Oblivion ne'er o'erthrows!"
　Meanwhile the stern Death-Angel with his sword
　Stood boldly forward to confirm my word.

———:o:———

THE OBLIVION OF THE PAST.

I.

THE brightest Suns will set at last,
　And Night usurp the realm of Day!
Where then the memory of the Past?—
　In dark Oblivion swept away.

II.

The myriad changes Earth hath seen
　Through myriad ages pass unknown;
And not a gleam of what hath been
　Disturbs the deep Oblivion.

III.

We see the effect—'tis plain to view—
　But seek in vain to find the cause;
Historic lore we ponder through
　In quest of Nature's hidden laws.

IV.

Whate'er we see—whate'er we are—
　Slow Process formed from things that were;—
But what that Process? Near and far,
　We seek—obtain—believe—but err!

V.

Thus to our doom we stand resigned
  Like myriads earlier ages bore ;
Oblivion hovers o'er mankind,
  Whose memory dwells on Earth no more.

VI.

But when I tuned my youthful lyre
  To sing of "dark Oblivion,"
The jarring crowds let loose their ire,
  And bade the echoes die unknown.

VII.

Vain man ! why seek to shun the doom
  That ev'n o'erhangs the pendent Earth ?
Oblivion Time cannot illume
  O'erhangs all things of mortal birth.

VIII.

The universe with fire aflame,
  Still drives ahead the realm of Day ;
But lo ! Death and Oblivion claim
  Their prey—and worlds dissolve away !

IX.

New worlds arise, and old ones die ;
  Thought—mind—and action quit their clay ;
And dark Oblivion hovers nigh.
  To end the memory of their sway !

X.

What then remains upon the cast
  When Life's eventful dream is o'er ?
An echo answers through the Past,
  "We have Oblivion—but no more ! "

Let Oblivion Rest.

I.

STIR not the ashes of Oblivion ;
  Lest from her dark sepulchral caves of woe,
Arise remembrances of days agone,
  Hateful and void.   There many an ancient throe
  Invites redress.   There Time destroys the foe,
    And smites the leman with his equal rod :
    Then let Oblivion rest beneath the sod.

II.

There dwell a thousand fantasies of youth
  O'er which repentant tears were poured as rain ;
There gazed upon, the sad remains of Truth
  Gleam with a spectral light !   The ancient bane
  Of happiness converts all joy to pain –
    And dread—and torment :—O how far 't were best
    To let the ashes of Oblivion rest !

III.

When anned, the ashes of Oblivion
  Ascend the skies, and draw the veil of Night
O'er many a scene where Memory, now o'erthrown,
  Adds double terror to the ruined sight :—
  And what the effect ?   To cast a gleaming light
    On ruined hate and love !   O then be wise :
    Bid not the ashes of Oblivion rise.

IV.

Not ev'n a remnant of Oblivion
  But teems with something hateful to the sight
Of Memory dim, when once 'tis overthrown,
  And re-instated.   'Tis the voice of Night
  That bids Oblivion cast a gleaming light
    On man's estate.   Yea, Nature's rule is best—
    Bury the Past, and let Oblivion rest.

V.

The serpent's curse is to survive on dust ;
  Such food for man was never wholesome yet ;

O ,hen why seek to chew the hated rust
  Of old Oblivion?   When he Sun is set
  Of Memory why endeavor to beget
    A falser light?   Ne'er to disturb her throne,
  Let man recede from dark Oblivion.

VI.

The ebon portals of Oblivion
  Entomb the ruined wrecks of centuries;
Her curtains hide the seats of empires known
  To ancient monarchs, when the troubled skies
  Shook with the clash of arms:—Can sacrifice
    Of toil be recompensed in the dark East,
    Where man contemns to let Oblivion rest?

VII.

What vast resources spent on ancient Troy,
  Long overthrown in dark Oblivion,
Where Greek and Trojan can no more annoy
  Each other and heap death on every stone,
  Could better be applied!   Long overthrown,
    Her very ruins are lost:—Let Troy attest
    What wisdom bids—and let Oblivion rest.

VIII.

Little we reck of Hector's matchless might,
  Or Helen's vanishment, or Troy's o'erthrow,
Or Ajax or Ulysses whom to fight
  The Trojan heroes oft to field did go;
  It rather now behooves mankind to know
    Of present States and kings.   The present call
    Invites to work—and bids Oblivion fall.

IX.

O dread Oblivion! rest thy mortal veil
  On whatsoe'er thou hast declared thine own!
Thine empire to thyself!   Let none assail
  Thy ebon walls!   Whatever be o'erthrown,
  'Tis vain to seek in dark Oblivion;—
    Confused sight!   Oblivion in unrest!
    Learn wisdom then—and let Oblivion rest!

The Vision of Oblivion.

I STOOD upon the rocks of Night—the rocks
  Which overhang the troubled sea of dark
Oblivion—and the mighty deep gave shocks
  Against the eternal hills;—and not an ark
Broke 'gainst the breakers of that vast Sublime
  Whose billows roar in thunder to the skies.
And overflow the records of old Time
  'Graved on the eternal rocks where ruin lies!
Before me rolled an ocean wild and waste,
  The troubled sea of dark Oblivion,—
The universal center whither haste
  Systems and States, confused and overthrown
In ruin! There Disaster reigns supreme,
  And Darkness like a pendent cloud of woe
Engenders blackest round the living stream
  Of far-historic lore. In overthrow,
Full many a tower by warrior-monarchs built
  To teach the future where the felon Past
In battle met, and where the blood was spilt
  Of Innocence—in ruins overcast—
Reared high above the flood, uplifted far
  Though fallen! Within that vasty realm of Night
Stood pre-historic and historic War.
  Confusing records never seen aright
By mortal eye. Save that a light Divine
  Finds secret way into the gazer's soul
No light appears! The ocean hath its line,
  The border whence its waves no further roll
Tumultuous;—but that dark Lethean flood
  No border knows! The myriad-rolling years
Reveal the horrid truth, though stained with blood,
  That Death, with horror plumed to shake the spheres,
But spreads the path for dark Oblivion
  With all its horrors.
               On the shore I stood
Of that tumultuous sea, to gaze upon
  The ruins rising through the angry flood.
And in the midst of that tumultuous flood

Isaiah, like a pyramid of flame—
Ezekiel—Daniel—Jeremiah—stood
For ever set upon the rocks of Fame,
 And shouting loud, a voice undimmed by years,
'Graved on the Sacred Page.
      Ev'n as the Sun
His blazing throne above the Atlantic rears
 In central skies—his highest zenith won—
And sheds his light on Europe and the shore
 Of Afric—evening rays, and on the coast
Of proud Columbia, far beyond the roar
 Of raging seas and monarchs tempest-tossed—
The morning rays! so blazing back and forth,
 The famed prophets with their visions cast
A flood of light—the light of all the earth—
 That fills alike the future and the Past
With wonder. Years on years shall roll along,
 And Dynasties beneath the sword expire,
And all things change;—and still the sons of Song
 Shall shake the world as with a rod of fire!
Theirs is the perpetuity of fame
 Which War can never give, though often sought
Upon his field. Ev'n so the prophet's name,—
 The name that moulds a world of living thought,
Blending alike upon the Sacred Page
 The Future and the Past.—But now my song
Has struck the rocks of Peace:—but why engage
 To thread it further through the mists of wrong
And right and doubt, in vision from the rocks
 Of Night—the rocks which overhang the sea
Oblivion—where the mighty deep gives shocks
 Against the eternal hills—eternally?

PART THIRD.

E M M E T .

I.

EUROPE had begun to tremble;
  Bonaparte was overthrowing
Ancient customs, rights and nations,
And with iron arm was strewing
Far around his bloody stations
Ruins of empires fierce and rudely.
Ireland—long oppressed and sorely—
Rose to war with her oppressors;
Raised the sword and swung it boldly
That her sons might be possessors
Of her castles, towers and steeples—
That her flag might wave in triumph
O'er her own, her ransomed people.

II.

Emmet—Ireland's bravest hero—
Rode in triumph, clad in glory
Won on many a field of slaughter
Dearly bought and fiercely gory;
But his triumph soon abated,
And the cause he had defended
Perished;—while his life of valor
On an English gallows ended.
Life he spent in bold adventures
Fraught with danger and commotion;
Death he met in all his terror,
Yet expressed no strange emotion;

E'en beneath the cursed halter—
Patriotism alone inclined him—
Loud he spoke without a falter
Cheering those he left behind him:
"One request I leave behind me:
When my country takes her station
With the States of fame and glory,
An emancipated nation
Proud to tell her ancient story;
When the Saxon's power is smitten;—
Then my comrades—*not until then*—
Let my epitaph be written!"

III.
Closed his eyes of radiant beauty;
Ceased his tongue to speak for Freedom;
Bowed his soul;—as to his duty
Hasted England's hangman rudely.
Moments endless in duration
Passed along; wild consternation
Seized the throng; in vast commotion—
Wild and dread—the storms of ocean
Howled for vengeance round the nation!
Soon the tragic scene was ended;
Dangling 'neath the cursed gibbet,
'Twixt the Heavens and earth suspended,
Died an advocate of Freedom!
Loud the shrieks of lamentation
Burst from hearts that would not weary;
And the notes of condemnation
Echoed through the Irish nation
Joyous lately, henceforth dreary.
Freedom wept with tears of sorrow;
Despotism rejoiced with smiling;
Ireland—trembling for the morrow—
Gave him up. The grave had won him!
Ended were his days of labor
With the pike, the spear, the saber;
And his name forever graven
On the temple-spires of Glory
Had immortalized his nation.
Now he sought a silent haven
In the tomb—his future station—
With the silent clods upon him!

IV.

Long he's lain—and yet is lying—
In his tomb, an Irish martyr ;
Still his countrymen are trying
Vainly to retrieve their station ;
Still his name is held unsullied
By the free of every nation.
Others' names may lose their luster ;
Others' acts as soon as ended
Cease to be with glory blended ;
But whene'er the patriots muster,
Emmet's praise shall be the anthem ;
Emmet's name shall catch new praises,
Crown the spires that Freedom raises ;
Thus through countless scenes and phases,
Live forever—Freedom's Glory's—
Blent with thousand martyr stories !

———:o:———

ARNOLD.

I.

LOOK on him in his fallen state,
   Rejected, scorned and cast aside
By those with whom he fought of late,
And rode to victory side by side !
An outcast from his land of birth !
A vagabond upon the earth !
A piteous wreck of youthful fame!
The ruins of a cherished name!

II.

What made him thus ?   Has virtue failed
To give rewards by merit earned ?
Not so—at least in his sad case—
For treachery thus he's scoffed and spurned !
To this he sacrificed his name !
To this surrendered all his fame !
For this received a bag of gold !
His birthright, ere 'twas gained, was sold !

JUDAS MACCABEUS.

O FOR a thousand tongues to sing the praise
Of Maccabeus who in darker days
Than mediæval freed the Church of God
From foul oppression of the Syrian rod—
From small beginnings paved his way to fame —
'Mid War's alarms immortalized his name—
Upreared the State and Church so long oppressed—
And died with heathen lances in his breast!
The Fourth Antiochus o'erblown with pride—
With Jupiter Olympias as his guide—
O'erran Judea ; slew her sons in fight,
And re-erected there the powers of Night ;
Ransacked the Temple—braving Power Divine—
And sprinkled blood thereon and broth of swine!
These crimes Jehovah from his throne surveyed
And wrested victory from the Heathen blade ;
And Maccabeus on the change of Fate
Redeemed the Church—upreared the fallen State—
And clothed with honor, wisdom and renown,
Supreme y ruled without the royal crown.
The proud successes of the rising State
Stirred up the Heathen to their ancient hate,
And brutal War o'erran the Glorious Lands ;
Proud Apollonius—Lysias—the bands
Of ancient Edom—and the Arab train—
And thousands others fought—but fought in vain ;
A Power unseen the Hebrew conqueror led
Who rode triumphant o'er the Heathen dead,
Restored Jehovah's service long profaned,
And in the midst of wild commotions reigned.
Thus Maccabeus carved his honored name
Triumphant on the temple-spires of Fame,
Where still it shines the noblest of its kind,
A monumental record undefined.
Nor was his death less glorious than his life—
His death that sprung from out the Heathen strife ;
He met the Heathen armies, gave them fight,
And drove them back through slaughter to the height

Of far Azotus where as by mischance
He met grim Death a-jousting with his lance !
Thus ends the most illustrious warrior's life
That ever figured on the fields of strife;
That Judas fell whose proud and daring name
Shines brightest on the scrolls of ancient Fame.

———:o:———

At the Grave of Napoleon.

I.

THIS is his grave—tread lightly o'er him !
    Earth's mightiest scepter once he swayed,
And bore a name ne'er borne before him ;
    But now he in the dust is laid !

II.

Born in an age of revolutions,
    He soon became inured to war
Where, marking Fortune's evolutions,
    He proudly placed his royal car.

III.

On many a field far-famed and gory
    Where Nations in a twinkling died,
Inured to fame and wrapped in glory,
    He rode with Victory side by side.

IV.

Pride filled his heart with stern ambition
    That mean se·vility disdained
And raised him to his high position
    Where as a warrior-prince he reigned.

V.

But Fate decreed that St. Helena
    Should be his seat in exile life ;
He went; and Death with his subpœna
    Called round and summoned him from strife !

VI.

Proud warriors now may rush to battle
    And fight till blood as rivers runs ;
But he no more can hear the rattle
    Of swords and helmets, spears and guns !

ᏟADE'S ᎡEBELLION.

I.

ᎡEBELLION raised her Hydra head,
  And through the south of England spread
Her fatal bane, a flaming ire
To overwhelm the ancient realm
And strew the world with blood and fire;
    And many a warrior proud and brave
    Chose rather *death* then be a-*slave !*

II.

The Rebel flag was hoisted high;
The shout for battle tore the sky;
The warrior decked his ancient plume;—
When General Cade picked up his blade
Resolved to make a gory tomb
    His final harbor—so he spoke—
    Or free his comrades from the yoke.

III.

With ponderous arms for bloody strokes
He marched his troops to Sevenoaks
And put to rout a Royal force;
Then raising high the battle cry
Toward London bent his fatal course !
    He hoped to gain ere set of sun,
    The Tower, the city and the throne !

IV.

Undaunted marched the Rebel band
With General Cade who sword in hand
Lead on, and in an evil hour,
With his baton smote London Stone
And cried, "The city's in my power !"
    He fearless seemed of living might,
    And felt as at Ambition's he ght.

V.

But when the Royal Guard advanced
To greet him with the sword and lance;
Our hero found his warriors fled !

Then in disguise he shunned surprise
In hopes to save his traitorous head—
    But all in vain !   He soon was caught,
And his rebellion came to naught !

————:o:————

GUITEAU.

I.

AMID the peace of twenty years,
    Inspired by man's eternal foe,
'Twas he who mingled blood with tears,
    And struck the pride of nations low ;

II.

When lo ! the myriad wires aflame
    To earth proclaimed the heinous crime,
And graved the proud assassin's name
    For ever on the page of Time.

III.

And Safety trembled on her throne—
    And Valor for awhile was dead !
And Justice calling loud and long,
    Demanded judgment on his head.

IV.

Yet Time hath rarely failed to blow
    The trump of doom where crimes abound ;
The eternal law works ever slow,
    Yet in its turn is Justice found.

V.

And thus the stern assassin's name
    Shall " thundering through the ages go ;"
But who'll applaud his zealous aim
    When he shall try the strength of tow ?

VI.

For Justice hovers o'er his head,
    And shouts his doom, and spurns control :
" Thou shalt be hanged till thou art dead !
    And God have mercy on thy soul ! "

THE CRIME OF GUITEAU.

I.

"STALWART President!" he cried ;
"I 'll do it for the God !" and shot ;
The while his victim laughed aside,
    And knew it not.

II.

And fifty million people mourn
The loss of him they love so well ;
And o'er the festal boards is heard
    The funeral knell.

III.

No war had roused men's fiery hearts ;
A peace of twenty years prevailed ;—
When with the fury hate imparts,
    The fiend assailed.

IV.

Now let the stricken world retire,
And put her mourning garments on ;
The life which ev'n his foes admire
    Will soon be gone !

V.

Bright were his glories to the last ;
He fell a martyr at his post ;
His star which set into the Past
    Is not all lost.

VI.

But where's the fiend that fired the shot ?
Shall he, like Booth, escape?—Ah no !
Policemen seize him on the spot,
    And cry, " Don't go !"

VII.

" Be still, my friends !" the assassin cries ;
"I want to go to jail !" O Time !
When was such impudence combined
    With such a crime ?

VIII.

O had they dealt Ravaillac's doom,
Full half his crime had not been known !
His blasphemy deserved no tomb
     . Or mercy shown.

IX.

Was e'er such infamy outdone?
The God to bear a Guiteau's crime !
So shall his declarations run
     To latest time.

X.

And shall the God endure the blame,
And free the murderer from his crime?
Ah no ! The felon bears the shame
     To latest time.

XI.

His inspiration fails in court ;
Such barbarisms no longer awe ;
For Justice cries aloud and short,
     "Avenge the law !"

———:o:———

GRAY.

SWEET GRAY ! how could thy wife forbear
    To love thee ?—At thy sacred tomb
May builders of the lofty rhyme
    At leisure read their awful doom ?
Thy verse inspired the heart of Wolfe
    At Quebec gazing o'er the height ;
Yea, world applauded Webster heard
    Thy strains in death and cried, " That's right !"
How then could filial love be slack
    To pour upon thy head its balm ?
Thou sweetest bard of thousand years,
    Who gave to Elegy her palm !
Sweet Gray ! thy memory still is clear ;
    Thy strains what mortal can forget ?
A world still gazes on thy bier,
    And mourns that such a sun could set.

THE DEATH OF PIZARRO.

I.

A CONQUEROR clothed with wreaths of ancient fame,
  A traitor stained with villainy and disgrace,
An heir of fortune and a son of shame,
Undaunted stood Pizarro in his place
      When rushing up the stair
      Herrada's band declare,
" Long live the king, but let the tyrant die !"
      In tones that shake the sky,
      And bring before the mind
      The cruelties refined
    That had disgraced the Spaniard's power
    And ushered in the direful hour
When vengeance stirs the hearts of men to ire
To rush o'er pools of blood and beds of fire.

II.

In days agone the penalty of death
Pizarro poured with a relentless hand
On Peru's inca who resigned his breath
A strangled martyr to his native land,
      Though as a ransom set
      Before he "paid the debt,"
He filled with gold his spacious prison cell !
      Next great Almagro fell
      A victim to his ire ;
      But now revenge as fire
    Heats up the proud conspirers' hearts
    Who with a zeal that hate imparts
Rush up the stairway shrieking loud the cry,
" Long live the king, but let the tyrant die !"

III.

Pizarro calls for arms and 'gins to deal
Untiring strokes at his relentless foes
Who capapie in armor scorn to feel
The double dint of his unerring blows ;
      His comrades one by one
      Heave forth the parting groan—

Yet still he holds his murderers to the fight
   Who glorying in their might
   And sworn to win the day,
   Thrust back and stab their prey
Full in the throat! then rushing down
The bloody stairs, proceed to drown
The clamorous uproar with the horrid cry,
" Long live the king, but let the tyrant die !"

———:o:———

THE COUNT PULASKI.

I.

THE stars of Freedom from her flag unfurled
   Shone eastward (as Columbian lore relates ;)
The groans of Freedom echoed round the world,
And lured heroic hearts from distant States ;
   Among the same Pulaski came.

II.

Where dangers hovered thickest round the post,
Where shot and shell disturbed the realm of air,
His men pure heroes and himself a host,
By valor led through thickest clouds of war
   Like lightning flew Pulaski's crew.

III.

Thus rolled the war through many a fateful day
And many a clime, till 'mid its clamors loud
Grim Death arrived to carry off his prey
From far Savannah where in battle proud
   'Mid storms of shell Pulaski fell !

IV.

Though dead to Earth, his honored name survives,
Deep 'graven on the registers of Time ;
And those from whom he tore the Feudal gyves
Revere his memory. Thus in fame sublime
   That valor gives Pulaski lives !

THE CRIME OF BOOTH.

I.

"SIC semper tyrannis!" he cried;
　"Virginia is avenged!" and fled
Through the wild crowds that stood beside
　　The murdered dead.

II.

Not since the dark and barbarous days
Of old had Villainy performed
A bloodier deed ;— with wrath ablaze
　　The plot he formed.

III.

The great Rebell on in the States
Was o'er ; the Cannon's roar was dead ;
And Peace stood smiling in the gates
　　Where Valor bled ;—

IV.

When lo! the Assassin arms in hand
Springs to the box that Lincoln filled,
And starts the echo through the land,
　　"The sage is killed !"

V.

To make defense was now too late ;
The murderer took his aim and shot ;
And Lincoln yielding to his fate
　　Fell on the spot !

VI.

The murderer then with nimble speed
Leaped from the box that fatal night,
And crying, " Virginia is avenged !"
　　Made good his flight.

⌐AFAYETTE IN ⌐RISON.

I.

⌐ARK is my dungeon cell—no light—
No rest—no hope again to roam
The paths of youth—no friend but Night!
  Is this my doom?

II.

O Freedom! why art thou so lost
To power—to honor—and to fame?
Has man not paid the dreadful cost
  With tears and shame?

III.

Alone I sit in deepest Night—
Tyrannic Night that dims the soul!
What can a tyrant breed but Night?
  Is this my goal?

IV.

Olmutz! thou dread and withering name!
Immortal infamy—infernal Night—
Barbaric hate—eternal shame—
  Be thy delight!

————:o:————

⌐ASHINGTON.

A FRAGMENT OF THE AUTHOR'S FIRST POEM.

⌐E carved his name
  On the temple of Fame
By living true;
May we not like him
Though our chance looks dim
Carve one there too?

.

Death of Louis XVI.

I.

THE gazing crowds tumultuous stood;
  The scaffold felt unusual weight;
The Sixteenth Louis with his blood
  Stood forth a sacrifice of State!

II.

The charge to beat the drums was given;
  Loud cried the priest amid the roar,
" Son of Saint Louis, ascend to Heaven!"
  And soon the tragic scene was o'er.

III.

The quick-descending guillotine
  Asunder cut the mortal thread;
And Louis Capet—France's king—
  No longer wore his royal head!

————:o:————

Mahomet.

SHALL stern Mahomet pass unsung?—A thousand years
    of blood
Point out to future ages where the prophet-monarch stood;
A soldier on the field of Mars, a monarch on the throne—
What marvel if his statutes live, engraved as on a stone?
A priest beside the altar-place, a prophet in the cave—
What marvel if his worship turn the freeman into slave?
A vasty wheel he set in motion reaching to the skies,
Then fell asleep forever—but his great examples rise;
A thousand years this whirling wheel of empire set to work
To aid the Asiatic hordes—the Saracen and Turk;
While roared the war on every hill where ancient Freedom
    stood,
And banded nations yelled the shouts that filled the world
    with blood!

PART FOURTH.

———∞◇∞———

THE PRELUDE.

I.

ONCE more upon the fields of rhyme
  Ye find me in an auxious race,
Aud spurring toward the true sublime
  My jaded Pegasus apace.

II.

But how my song the public ear
  Will greet, 'tis needless to inquire ;
For who can sing from year to year,
  Yet find no foes to mock his lyre ?

III.

Yet some will love the strains I know,
  Whose souls, like mine, have racked and torn,
And like the raven seen by Poe,
  One melancholy burden borne.

IV.

To those, and others who will stay
  To hear, I pour my present song;
The speed that urges won't delay
  While Pegasus can jog along.

THE REIGN OF LOVE.

I.

I STOOD awhile to gaze upon the Past,
  And to recall the scenes beloved of yore;
And as I gazed upon the vision vast,
  Fond Memory led where Truth had reigned before;
    And as I stood adoring ancient Truth,
    Love throned himself upon the throne of Youth.

II.

And when I wandered where the fateful dart
  Of Danger waged a tireless war on Youth,
Lo! Love stood forth to shield my trembling heart,
  And guide me in the path of ancient Truth;
    Thus Love began to woo my youthful heart
    That yielded soon to his persuasive art.

III.

But oh! what awful change with later years!
  Love reigned a tyrant on the throne of Youth,
And drenched his rising State with needless tears,
  And ushered on the doubly-dreaded Truth—
    For Love's proud State cannot withstand the jar
    That his excesses give—but falls afar.

IV.

And oh! what awful state of needless woe!
  Love fought the battles with unerring might,
But fled his state in ruinous overthrow,
  When peace returned—and gave it o'er to Night!
    'Mid scenes of sweetness Love still sighed for more,
    And fled at last—to seek a purer shore?

V.

Now fades celestial music on the ear,
  And Death and Danger fly to scenes afar;
And having naught to hope and naught to fear,
  Love takes his flight—ev'n like a falling star!
    Or like a tree when winds have ceased to blow,
    O'erturns itself in ruinous overthrow!

THE DESTINY.

I.

DARK is my life—no light—no sun—
My day of usefulness is done!
I look upon a life misspent,
And note the joys that came and went,
And mourn the loss of Long Ago;
Alas, that love e'er made me so!

II.

Once I was happy in my youth,
And youthful love;—alas! the truth—
The woful truth—was simply this—
I truly loved, but loved amiss!
With loss of bliss I'm heir to woe;
Alas, that love e'er made me so!

III.

Could I not wean myself of love?—
As well to mount the skies above,
And fight the gods upon their seat,
As fight with Cupid or retreat;
Or stand or fall, ours is the blow;
Alas, that love e'er made me so!

IV.

Our will we must resign to Fate;
For we can never—till too late —
Discern the storms that wreck the skies;
'Tis thus with love! The watery eyes
Grow dim—then love is lost we know;
Alas, that love e'er made me so!

V.

I cannot hate my love, though she
Delights my wretchedness to see;
I know her love at first was true—
'Tis often thus when love is new—
But now, 'tis lost with Long Ago;
Alas, that love e'er made me so!

VI.

I'd fly away and be at rest;
But something hovers in my breast—
A wicked hope—'tis weakness though,
That prompts the hope I cling unto—
A hope that still forbids to go;
Alas, that love e'er made me so!

VII.

Could I recall my youth again,
I'd never herd with hated men,
But dwell a hermit in some cave,
And knowing none, no love would crave;
But youth—alas—is all aglow;
Alas, that love e'er made me so!

VIII.

Ah me! if Cupid would but deal
His blow with Fortune's, human weal
Would create envy in the gods!
Alas! by more than mortal odds,
Mine is the deepest love below;
Alas, that love e'er made me so!

————:o:————

To Jealousy.

RETIRE! thou most infernal thought,
With Satan's mischief doubly fraught!
No longer dare surround me;
Let all thy Hellish powers depart!
Thy poison take from out my heart,
So love can shine around me:—
Without thee Earth were Heaven indeed;
Then take thy flight with quickest speed!

My Love! forgive this fiery mood,
And help to quench this fiend of good;
Don't let it tear my heart from thee,
And plant a Hell where Heaven should be!

To Victoria.

MY home—which gloweth with solitude;
  My life—which knoweth no quietude;
My tongue—which soon shall cease to move!
My heart—the fallen throne of Love;
My mind—where joys were wont to roll,
And fill with rapture all my soul—
All—all as well might cease to be,
Since driven in despair from thee,
           I fled!
O wild despair! All hope is dead,
And waves of tumult roll instead!
My home had always solace given,
When by Despair my heart was riven;
So homeward all my thoughts inclined,
As oft as trouble crossed my mind.
And when the only heart I loved
Revealed its will, its coldness proved,
For solace quickly home I flew;—
Alas!—mistaken—all untrue!
To live was death! but oh, to die!
Dark, horrid clouds—I knew not why—
O'erspread throughout my moral sky!
Till then my life no trouble knew,
And had not still—hadst thou been true;
O cursed spot! How dread the place
Where Trouble first unveiled his face,
And from his horrid visage blew
The word that rived my heart in two:—
O deadly word! Soon as 'twas spoke,
Despair my aspirations broke
And life and joy with crushing stroke!
My heart, o'erfull with love, was thine,
And hoped that thine were truly mine;
But now it is asunder riven!
Hope and Despair have ceaseless striven
To gain therein the topmost seat;
But oh! love's trampled 'neath thy feet!
Despair shall be my winding sheet!

My mind was full of visions bright
That at thy bidding took their flight ;—
But now farewell.   Thy game is o'er
Forever and forevermore !

————:o:————

Restlessness.

I.

ONE month?   No, hardly three weeks yet,
   But seems an age twice told and more
Since last I left her father's door
         And on my journey set !
To me the same—when dark, when light—
While I'm so restless day and night !

II.

A school- -if school it might be called—
At Sinking-Ground I teach by day ;
At night I take my lonely stray
         To trouble deep inthralled ;
Sometimes for miles I take my flight
Because I'm restless day and night !

III.

And oh ! what book or poem now
Can soothe my mind or give it ease
While strolling lone 'mid rocks and trees,
         I pass time—who knows how ?—
For nothing now can please my sight,
I've got so restless day and night !

IV.

I might enlarge but deem it not
Of interest to the world or me ;
Suffice to say I hope to be
         One day upon the spot
Where stands my love with look so bri ght,
And then be restless day nor night !

ON NEW YEAR'S DAY.

I.

ALL hail, New year! Farewell, thou Old!
  To me the same both Old and New!
Your joys—your woes—are manifold;
  Your joys are only known to few.

II.

And Time, with broad and darkening wing,
  Has ushered in another year;
And Death, with cold and mortal sting,
  Prepares the Old one for the bier.

III.

Another year its doom has met;
  O'erthrown, it yields to Time at last;
The Sun that lit the year is set
  Beyond the mountains of the Past.

IV.

And when upon the scene I gaze,
  The ruins wrought throughout the year,
And think upon my earlier days,
  I tremble--yet I scorn the tear.

V.

For why should my once throbbing heart
  That laughed to scorn the fall of Youth,
Be broken by Disaster's dart,
  Or melted at the sight of Truth?

VI.

Oft have I felt the tyrant stroke
  Of Fate, and deeply mourned the blow;
But never yet my spirit broke,
  Or failed to bear its load of woe.

VII.

O had I gazed on what I saw,
  Nor thought to make it all my own,
I might have fancied bliss or awe,
  But both had still remained unknown.

VIII.

'To gaze had never broke the spell
 That hangs o'er Love's eternal throne ;—
But why forbear the truth to tell?
 I touched—the rapture all was gone !

IX.

Since that all-nameless hour of Fate,
 I live my natal day to curse ;
And though Disaster rears his State,
 It cannot make my torture worse !

X.

And yet some solace still I find
 In pondering past and present woe ;
For every sting that haunts the mind
 Portrays its power to stand the blow !

XI.

Then be each season like the last ;
 Though shorn of every other light,
Still let me gaze upon the Past,
 And learn to read the book of Night.

XII.

And now, while falls the dying Year
 Beneath the scythe of ancient Time,
I mourn—but scorn the useless tear—
 For all it brought—its good, its crime.

XIII.

Thus year by year the hopes of Youth
 Still perish with their year of birth ;
The rising year shall bear the truth
 To many a scene bereft of worth.

XIV.

Then hail, New Year ! Farewell, thou Old !
 To me the same both Old and New !
Your woes are truly manifold ;
 Your joys are only known to few !

At the Close of Day.

I.

AT twilight when the dusk of eve
Comes stealing slow but sure around,
I pause to think—who would believe?—
And fail to note above the ground
A single blessing not effaced ;
A single action not misplaced ;
One pure word either thought or spoken ;
And then my heart is almost broken !

II.

Then comes a dim remembrance felt
So oft when on the patient's bed
I lay almost unconscious and
My friends gave o'er and thought me dead ;
A feeling close akin to pain ;
A feeling fraught with stern disdain ;
While treacherous Memory only brings
A mass confused of broken things !

III.

Whate'er I see around me seems—
Not quite, but nearly so—the same
As something else that in my dreams
Of long ago both went and came ;
Or something nearly like what I
Have seen before ;—around me lie
The broken fragments—torn amain—
Of Love and Hate, and Joy and Pain !

IV.

O Joy ! thou art a word misplaced ;
O Pain ! in thee my soul survives ;
O Hate ! with horrors thou art graced ;
O Love ! with thee my spirit strives !
Without thy rays of genial light
Earth's brightest days were deepest nigh :
Unless thy sovereign power control,
Woe to the most aspiring soul !

V.

He that hath never felt thy power,
At best is but a sluggish beast;
Let no such man e'en for an hour
Be trusted—no, not in the least!
His heart is cold as Polar ice;
His keenest virtue is a vice;
His soul broods in Plutonian night
And shudders at the thoughts of light!

VI.

But oh! dread Memory breaks the chain
Of Love, and bids my spirit soar
Back to the times most fraught with pain
And paints them brighter than before;
Times long ago with sorrow fraught,
By treacherous Memory now are brought
In borrowed colors to portray
The distance I have fallen to-day!

————:o:————

TIMBERLEE.

I.

AND Timberlee has got a wife,
The present joy of future life!
Successful in his wooings past
He brings her to his home at last;
And Love is all the law they have,
And each is still the other's slave!
   O Timberlee! O Timberlee!
   If I were you how glad I'd be!

II.

A year has passed:—their joys are dead!
Their hours of pleasure all have fled!
They gaze each other's face the while—
Yea gaze—and gaze—but cannot smile!
For Love has fled his pearly throne,
And weeping now cannot atone!
   O Timberlee! O Timberlee!
   If I were you how sad I'd be!

To a Sweet Singer.

I.

E'V'N as the voice of Nature's Sire
    That hushed the waves of Galilee,
So sounds upon the heart's deep lyre,
    The music of thy voice to me.

II.

So sweet the melody serene
    Floats o'er the spirit's vision wide,
I seem as borne afar, between
    An angel's voice on either side.

III.

And when thou singst of Beulah Land,
    And setst thy flaming eyes on me,
Save that I may not touch thy hand,
    Love's Paradise were full in thee!

IV.

But oh! the tear instinctive falls
    When Memory strikes her woful strain,
And Duty's well-known voice replies—
    " Depart—and ne'er return again !"

V.

Thus in the midst of music's charms,
    O'erruling Fate my doom decrees,
And bars me from thy loving arms—
    Where thou wouldst have me bask at ease !

VI.

And must I heed the stern decree,
    And fly like zenith's falling star?
" Farewell to Beulah Land and thee !"
    In notes of love resounds afar.

"I NE'ER SHALL SMILE AGAIN."

I.

THE moon was shining silver-bright
  Around the calm lagoon;
The oars were flashing in the light
  Like Zenith seen at noon:—
A youth advanced with careless step
  Adown the open glen,
Sighing anon with bated breath—
  " I ne'er shall smile again !"

II.

The noise of laughter on the lake
  Is fraught with radiant joy;
The faces of the youths partake
  A kind of sweet annoy :—
But oh ! the lad with folded arms
  Still pushes through the glen,
Sighing anon with heavy heart—
  " I ne'er shall smile again !"

III.

The voice of plighted love is heard
  Upon the lakelet's breast;
And lovers tremble at the word
  That fills them with unrest:—
The while that melancholy youth
  Still wanders o'er the glen,
Sighing anon the fatal truth—
  "I ne'er shall smile again !"

IV.

The voice of love upon the lake
  Is fraught with deep unrest;
The trembling lass begins to quake
  When first her lips are pressed !
The while that boy with bated breath,
  Cursed with the eternal bane,
Still sighs amid his living death—
  "I ne'er shall smile again !"

V.

The moon is sinking slow to rest
  Beyond the still lagoon ;
And lovers folded heart to breast
  Account their sorrows done :—
But oh ! what throbbings heave the breast
  Of him who sighs in vain,
And murmurs still as scorning rest—
  " I ne'er shall smile again !"

————:o:————

THE LOVER'S FAREWELL.

I.

'TIS o'er ;—I leave the realm of Bliss !
  Adieu ! ye joys too quickly flown ;
Adieu ! sweet rest forever gone ;
Adieu to Love's enamored kiss !
I now must fly—to lands unknown ;
Must dwell amid the throng—alone ;
Must dwell with those who know not bliss ;
Must fall asleep—without thy kiss !

II.

I flee ; but wheresoe'er I go,
With treacherous Memory still I'll strive
And in my visions keep alive
The fond embrace you now bestow !
For thee my love shall ever burn ;
For thee my heart shall beat return ;
With thee in love perpetual dwell ;
From thy advises ne'er rebel !

III.

And now farewell ! I will not choke
The sigh that rises to assure
Thy trembling heart that love is pure ;
Love trembles 'neath the parting stroke !
E'en in the tear survives relief ;
The artless tear insures belief ;
Wilt kiss ?—thy lips were ne'er more sweet !
Adieu ! sweet kisses—till we meet !

To My Betrothed.

I.

MOST lovely form of womankind—
  Most Heavenly maid of Earth!
Still let me in thy bosom find
  Love, happiness and worth;

II.

Let still thy love around me shine
  My weary soul to guide;
Permit me still to call thee mine—
  My loved—my future bride!

III.

Though foes may still my soul distress
  And strive my love to shake,
Yet if they hope to have success
  They labor through mistake.

IV.

If still thy love around me shines
  To calm Life's troubled roar,
Give quick anew thy tokening signs,
  And up my soul shall soar!

V.

But should thy love grow false to me
  My heart—no more my own—
In dark despair and gloom shall be
  Forevermore alone!

VI.

If Love with rays of power divine
  Hath warmed thy tender heart,
Hath blent thy heart and soul with mine
  And bid all else depart—

VII.

Doubt not that I sincere will prove;
  For all the world can see
That all my happiness and love
  Are jointly shared with thee!

VIII.

'Tis love for thee that shields my soul
From trouble's chilling blight;
And when I else would feel alone
Thy love sets all aright.

IX.

And many other works of Love
I might present to view,
But for the present I defer,
Since what I've said will do!

————:o:————

THE CURSE OF FATE.

. I.

SAW thee once, and thou didst steal
My heart—at least you thought 'twas mine—
Sweet rogue! my soul shall ever feel
Its deepest raptures at thy shrine:
I love thee? Yea, 'twere hard to tell
How long I've loved thee and how well—
But Fate allured to distant land,
And bade me never touch thy hand!

II.

O mystery of remorseless Fate!
Must I for ever mourn my lot?
Or shall I in some future state
Find my forbidden love forgot?
Thou hast my heart—but what's it worth?
My hand was barred from thee at birth;
The curse of Fate is ours for ever,
And I shall see thy face—ah—never!

The Autograph.

I.

MY life a mystic river is
  Whose course not ev'n its wavelets know ;
All scenes of happiness and bliss
  To me are ever haunts of woe.

II.

And now, though dazzling Beauty smiles,
  And Love, from his eternal throne,
Beckons to me through radiant eyes,
  Still must my heart beat still alone.

III.

For I can ne'er thy charms survey,
  Unawed by Youth's mistakes and Time's ;
And yet the truth will shine one day,
  And thou wilt slander me with crimes !

IV.

But why should I thus burden Youth
  With inward sorrows fit for Age ?
Or write through mysteries a truth
  To whelm thy softer heart with rage ?

V.

Yet peace to thee ! The vanished Past
  To dark Oblivion's pit consign :
The seal is set—the die is cast—
  I know my fate--thou know'st not thine.

VI.

And I must fly to lands afar,
  Where Duty's voice calls loud to me ;
The gate is standing now ajar,
  But I must not approach to thee !

THE DECLARATION.

THOUGH love-waves o'er my nature roll
And fill with rapture all my soul,
It ne'er hath been my lot to see
Her more devoutly loved by me
Than thou hast been and still shalt be!
Therefore my humble heart shall be
An offering of Love to thee!
Our long acquaintance speaketh well
Of friendsh p that caused some to tell
That I with thee in love had fell;
But still when speaking to thy face,
My pulse would run perpetual race—
Despair would veil my timid face—
My heart would tremble in its place—
My tongue –it too would cease to move
Whene'er I tried to speak of love!
" I'll talk of other things to-day,
And on to-morrow I will say
The words I've tried so much!"
My resolution many a time;
It seems to tell it is a crime!
Away—away with such!
I'd talk our whole acquaintance o'er,
And try to speak of Love once more,
To say a word it 'twere but one;
But silly tongue—it wouldn't run!
But now I've thrown my fears away!
Yet how I cannot tell;
Enabled now am I to say :
" My Dear! I love thee well ;
I love thee dearly, and to-night
My love is pure as snow is white !"

To an Early Friend

I.

SWEET girl! Though I may never see
The face that smiled so oft on me,
When in the happy days of youth,
We loved—but dared not own the truth—
Still shall my heart, at thought of thee,
Beat high—and struggle to be free!

II.

Through many a land 'tis mine to stray,
And curse my lot from day to day,
And seek for happiness in vain,
Since youth cannot return again ;—
Yet when I think of love and thee,
My heart still struggles to be free!

III.

But when thou hear'st that I have failed
To stem the tempests that assailed,
Let not those eyes be dimmed with tears
That sparkled so in earlier years;
Such tears—when shed by love and thee—
Would break my heart or make it free!

IV.

Is this our doom?—and yet I would
Not on thy tender heart intrude;
And now farewell ! No earthly joy
Hath yet been found without alloy;
My heart—once beating loud for thee—
Must beat in vain—no longer free!

THE POWER OF LOVE.

I.

I ASKED a sage with whom I met,
        "Your views of Love?"
His answer clings to memory yet:

II.

" A greater boon hath ne'er been given
        To man than Love,
By Him who sits enthroned in Heaven.

III.

" When Sorrow's darts fly thickest round,
        The shield of Love
A sure defense is always found.

IV.

"No burden e'er too heavy seems
        When rays of Love
From Love's own dazzling temple gleam.

V.

" The light and power and guide of Life
        Are found in Love
The conqueror of every strife.

VI.

" *Omnia vincit amor !*   All
        Succumb to Love
The conqueror of both great and small.

VII.

"Were I condemned to live on Earth
        Untaught by Love
I could but curse my hopeless birth."

VIII.

I turned and said : " My friend, 'tis true ;
        The power of Love
I've felt as far and deep as you."

To Time.

I.

ALAS is man! why dost thou overthrow
Our happiness ere we begin to know
Its worth and how to thwart thy mortal blow?
    O tyrant Time!

II.

Some happiness for all is yet in store;
And yet 'tis useless—thou art at the door
To wield thy rod as in the days of yore,
    O tyrant Time!

III.

'Tis thus that thou hast broken my poor heart
So joyous once! And canst thou not impart
Some blessing save thy all-devouring dart?
    O tyrant Time!

IV.

Our sweetest happiness is love of Truth
And sweetest Purity;—that thou in sooth
Dost scorn to leave at overthrow of Youth,
    O tyrant Time!

V.

And oh! 'tis mine to weep in sorrow sore
That thou hast robbed me thus, and to deplore
Thy needless tyranny forever more,
    O tyrant Time!

———:o:———

To Miriam.

WHEN other cares my mind employ
    And strive my thoughts from thee to wrest,
My heart within shall leap for joy
    At thought of her who loves me best;
        And feel full blest in being owned
        By Love within thy breast enthroned!

LOVE.

I.

IN every man by Nature bred
  Exist the principles of love ;
And yet how oft 'tis falsely said
  That Love is flown to realms above !

II.

Love has not fled the earth as yet,
  Though hard beset by sweating Lust ;
'Tis vain to think the sun is set
  Because a cloud obscures his trust.

III.

For round sweet Beauty's dazzling throne
  Of purest chastity and truth,
Love holds his revels all alone,
  And wallows in the lap of Youth.

IV.

'Twere better far to love in vain,
  Than let the spark of love expire !
Once dead, it ne'er revives again,
  But smothered most doth most aspire.

V.

The love of music and the love
  Of woman be my spirit's food,
Or moonlight stealing through the grove,
  By wicked woodsman unsubdued.

VI.

But let his soul be racked with pain
  Who strives the source of love to move,
Or cries unto his fellow man,
  " Scorn to the offices of Love !"

The Lover's Return.

I.

SWEETEST joys to mortals known!
  To meet with whom we love and not
To find one parting vision gone,
  The trembling, farewell look forgot!
Days into seconds crowd, and all
The visions of pure youth recall;
And Memory—traitorous still forsooth—
Hides faults, e'en at the expense of truth!

II.

Sweet Love! 'tis well for thee I live;
  I could not live untaught by thee!
Here all I am and have I give,
  An humble offering still for me!
With thee my heart shall ever beat;
From thee my spirit ne'er retreat;
To thee my soul for aye be given;
From thee my service ne'er be driven!

————:o:————

To My Absent Dove.

I.

THE last three months appear to me
  As but one summer day;
A day's an hour when I'm with thee—
  A month when I'm away!

II.

When thou receivest this to-morrow
  Peruse—reflect—and love;
Remember one whose only sorrow
  Is for his absent Dove!

ABSENCE.

I.

'TIS sweet on Memory's page to read
Of times that had no sweetness when
They flitted by with unknown speed
. And joined the Fathomless again ;
When at the study table met
By Love's own dazzling form I sat,
But felt unconscious of the light
That banished all the powers of Night !

II.

'Twas meet that I thus read the words
On record left by those who trod
The Earth in earlier ages and
Returned to life beneath the sod ;
I learned thereby the powers of mind,
The strongest of the strongest kind ;
I learned thereby the dreadful truth,
That Joy no partner is of Youth !

III.

But now far in the distance flung
I seek in vain life from the dead ; —
The harp beside me lies unstrung ;
The book beside me lies unread ;
Where'er the wanderer's path I roam,
Loom up remembrances of home,
And absence pours Plutonian night
Around the stream and source of light !

ON THE CLIFF.

I.

THE kiss of love—the love sick soul's delight—
 Who would exchange it for the wealth of gold?
Who so degenerate as to barter love
 For royalty—as in the days of old?

II.

Blind ignoramus! What else shall I say?
 Devil!—I'll say it though I fall thereby!
Fettered with night so near the source of day—
 What villain doubts that he deserves to die?

III.

And yet the woes of lovers are unknown,
 Save to the few experience calls by name—
Or what eternal horrors seize upon
 The heart that loves ere it attains its aim.

IV.

All have I felt;—and in its turn have felt
 What 'tis to love where fortune never shone!
And therefore am I weary now and sad—
 For love is lost—and I am left alone!

V.

O days of youth! I little understood
 The weal ye offered when upon the shore
Of Time's dread ocean I undaunted stood,
 And gazed—and pondered —shall I ponder more?

VI.

What I would recollect is soon forgot;
 What I would fain forget survives o'erthrow;
What most I dreaded is befallen my lot—
 And all my happiness is drowned in woe!

VII.

With less of youth I gained a woman's smile;
 With loss of peace I stand the crags above!
In face of Death I stand to gaze awhile
 The universal loss—of life and love!

VIII.

And ye who in the rugged vale below—
   A thousand feet below—my bones shall find,
Curse not the suicide until ye know
   The horrid flame that bade him shun mankind!

IX.

Is love a crime?—'tis all the crime I've done:—
   But death hath terrors worse than lovers' shocks!
Farewell ye sons of men!—and I have gone
   To be a brother to the insensible rocks!

————:o:————

LINES TO MIRIAM.

ON PRESENTING HER THE PICTURE OF A CROSS WITH A RING
FASTENED THEREON.

YOU see the cross? How firm it is!
   How sure the ring around it clings!
'Twill there remain when both are old—
Through damp and dry, through heat and cold—
For 't can't be loosed (as I am told ;)
So is my love to thee!
My love encircles round thee still,
Encircles now and always will!
O then why not love me?
When hands of thine are placed in mine,
Thy face like sunbeams o'er me shines ;
Thy countenance glad tidings brings.
My troubles all are changed to bliss,
When—sweetest of all—thy face I kiss!

The Farewell.

I.

O WHAT a world of pain and woe,
  Whose fatal poison none can tell,
Swells on the aching heart below
  And centers in the word " Farewell!"

II.

Joy hath no strain that sounds complete,
  Such sorrows round its closing dwell;
The joy of friends who gladly meet
  Dims at the hated word " Farewell!"

III.

Full many a scene we wholly hate
  Grows sweet at last and all is well;
And then we mourn the blasts of Fate
  And sigh to speak the word " Farewell!"

IV.

But why this heavy heart should mourn
  For aught on earth 'twere hard to tell;
And yet I would not thus be borne
  From scenes that ask a long " Farewell!"

V.

Oft have I heard the voice of Truth,
  And felt my soul with rapture swell;
But now to scenes like those of youth
  Must bid a longing last " Farewell!"

VI.

O world of pain! O world of woe!
  How deep thy poison none can tell;
The startling woes of Long Ago
  All center in the word " Farewell!"

The Epitaph,

I.

HIS Yonth did fail amid its prime
   When stern Unrest upreared his throne ;
And raving on the tyrant Time,
   He took his leave for parts unknown.

II.

Through this dark gate he coolly passed
   Unto a far and trackless realm,
Still gazing fondly on the Past
   While Death sat sternly at the helm.

III.

Without consent born to the earth,
   He took his leave e'en as he came ;
Small profit gained he by his birth ;
   'Twas but a parent's gift—a name '

PART FIFTH.

THE ATHEIST.

I.

WHEN o'er the Earth the tempest rolls
And fills with horror stoutest souls;
When from the Heavens the bolts descend
That jar the Earth from end to end;—
What man that walks the Terrene sod
Shall murmur forth, "There is no God!"

II.

When on the Earth in calmer days
The Sun pours forth his genial rays;
When nightly o'er the calm lagoon
Majestic floats the silent moon;—
What worm in shape of mortal clod
Shall dare to say, "There is no God!"

III.

When trembling at Jehovah's ire,
The Earth shall wrap herself in fire;
When through the vast expanse of Time
The Archangel's trump shall sound sublime;—
What awful doom for him that trod
The Earth and cried, "There is no God!"

THE HEREAFTER.

I.

LIFE is an isle betwixt the seas
Of two unknown Eternities—
An isle where hangs the sword of Death
Upon the workings of a breath !

II.

'Tie o'er ; and Love now tears the bier !
And Pity sheds the burning tear !
And human frailty cries aloud
Till echoed wails surround the shroud !

III.

Philosophy may vainly try
To soothe the grief for those who die ;
The passage still demands a tear
For all who press the silent bier !

IV.

Life rises high to soar and burst,
And turn to what it was at first !
But who shall pierce the mystic pall
To read the future doom of all ?

V.

And yet we know the final doom
Is far beyond the boasting tomb ;
There all shall fall, and all shall own
The presence of the "great Unknown !"

VI.

So live that when thy days are o'er,
And thou must glow with life no more,
A pangless conscience may illume
The dark recesses of the tomb !

VII.

For time is rolling on—and on—
And longest lives will soon be gone !
And little reck the present strife
Whom bright Hereafter calls to life !

THE THREATENERS.

I.

THE proudest knight
In armor bright
That ever met his foes in fight,
Could not withstand
The ghastly band
That threatens this illustrious land.

II.

With outstretched hands
On holiest lands
Proud ATHEISM the tyrant stands;
And like a swell
Proceeds to tell
His creed: " No God! No Heaven! No Hell!"

III.

Pale SKEPTICISM,
Dire ROMANISM,
The infidel " FREETHINKERISM,"
And myriads more
Stand at the door
Our foes as in the days of yore.

IV.

These we must meet
Or call retreat
Thereby insuring foul defeat;
For in the blaze
Of modern days
The astonished world the struggle weighs.

V.

Then Christians, rise!
Wait no surprise,
For valor unexerted dies;
Meet arms in hand
The ghastly band
That threatens this illustrious land!

THE IMPIOUS FARMERS.

I.

IN April when the showers of Spring
  Were frequent, boisterous and chill,
The neighboring farmers thought to bring
  Contempt upon the Almighty's will;
And argued long—but argued vain—
For more of sun and less of rain!

II.

Then ceased the rains, and for awhile
  All were delighted.   Herb and tree
Shook in the Sun's all-cheering smile;
  The earth was verdure; all was glee!
And neighbors when they met would say—
" Has any seen a prettier day ?"

III.

In June some wished a thunder-shower;
  Others desired a *silent* rain ;
While all put forth their utmost power
  To dress their fields—but all in vain !
The parched air was so deadly-hot
The earth was like a seething pot!

IV.

The drought in July still prevailed ;
  Not e'en a cloud adorned the sky !
Some prayed, some cursed, and some bewailed
  Their situation ; " We shall die
Of famine, pestilence and thirst !"
Cried thousands in that land accursed.

V.

In August blazed the parching Sun ;
  The solid earth to ashes turned ;
The race of life seemed well-nigh run !
  The fires prevailed ; the fields were burned ;
And in despair men rashly cried,
And thus the living God defied :

VI.

" Send down the rain !   No righteous God
   Could punish suffering mortals thus !
'Twere better far beneath the sod,
   Than to endure this hateful curse !
There is no God or he would deign
To send his suffering creatures rain !"

VII.

And when the equinoctial winds
   Athwart the parched horizon blew,
Cloud after cloud piled high in air ;
   The soaring bird toward Heaven upflew ;
And burst the tempest in its might,
And plunged the land in deepest Night !

VIII.

Tumultuous were the clouds around ;
   Tempestuous were the winds above ;
Harsh thunders shook the surging ground,
   And lightnings with each other strove ;
And earth it seemed had gone to wrack,
Or rolled from off her ancient track !

IX.

A river swelled from every rill
   And heaved the crested waves in air ;
Revolved the storm ! from every hill
   A torrent burst ; all was despair ;
And men with shattering voices cried,
" Save, Lord, from tempest, thunders, tide !"

X.

Then fled the clouds on winds reversed ;
   The thunders ceased ; the brightening Sun
Relit the day and quenched his thirst
   From useless floods whose charge was done !
From this let hasty grumblers learn
To take the weather in its turn.

THE PAPAL INTERDICT.

TREMBLE ye monarchs of a stricken world
   O'er whose domain the interdict is hurled !
Fling back the royalties of days agone ;
Fall in the dust and curse the fatal throne ;
For Papal vengeance wraps the world with fire,
And 'mid the wreck of nations heaves the pyre !
No more the farmer drives his teams afield ;
The farms no more their fruitful harvest yield ;
No more the housewife plies her evening care ;
And friends no more their mutual love declare ;
All Nature holds a universal gloom
While from the Eternal City rolls her doom :
" Ye proud opposers of the Church's power,
Ye who have ushered in this direful hour,
Howl ye and mourn !   Repent ye of your crimes !
Attempt no more to change the laws and times ;
Prostrate yourselves with faces toward the ground,
And beg for mercy while it may be found !
And ye on whom sedition hath no power,
Bring down the bell from the cathedral's tower ;
In shallow ditches bury all your dead !
The open heath declare your favorite bed ;
In church-yards celebrate the nuptial ties ;
Lay bare your heads beneath the cloudless skies ;
In mournful cadence weep the direful gloom ;
And ponder deep the horrors of the tomb,
Where, should ye fall beneath the Church's ire,
No hope remains but groans and penal fire !"

———:0:———

THE SCRIPTURES.

HOW strikingly Thy word portrays
   The present state, the final doom
Of all, when far in future days
   Beyond the tomb !

THE SHIP OF YOUTH.

I.

NOW let the youths of every land,
Who on the rocks of Danger stand,
Attend and listen to my song.
And learn to shun the giant Wrong
Which spreads around so many a lure
To make his own successes sure,
And hurries to a nameless grave
The sons of freedom and the slave.
And yet 'tis vain to sing the song
Of danger to the gaily throng
Who lift aloft the spark ing bowl
And drink this riot of the soul!
Who trust in Virtue's power to save,
And scorn the drunkard's early grave,
Yet like the progress of the Sun,
Whose course is slowly—surely—run,
Still pitch on each successive night
Their tent, and rear the beacon-light
A whole day's journey nearer Doom,
Nor once perceive the darkening gloom !
Yet will I sing the song of Life
That sailed so proud the seas of strife,
Till lured from off the charted line
And run to death by love of Wine !
And if the youth who hopes to be
A sailor on that living sea,
Will scorn this warning of the Past
And meet his folly's doom at last—
O let him with his parting breath
Tell whose the crime that brought him death !
And this—his doom—shall aid my song
That struggles with this giant Wrong
And warns the rising youth in time
To shun this poison bowl of Crime !

II.

The sky was clear as clear could be ;
And not a wave disturbed the sea !
And not a breeze beguiled the woods,
Or hushed the rushing of the floods !

The bay was like a sea of glass,
Reflecting from its crystal face
Each form of mountain-wood and rock
That reared itself, and seemed to mock
Imagination's wildest powers
And laugh to scorn her magic bower!
And oh! the prayers that then were said!
And oh! the tears that then were shed!
When first was launched—so wildly free—
The ship of Youth upon the sea,
And all its gallant crew began
To mingle in the ranks of man!
With many a promise—made in vain—
They launch upon the boundless main;
The straits of Manhood now are passed,
And Ocean meets the gaze at last!
So swift the vessel cuts the wave,
And surges from her liquid grave,
She walks the flood—a thing of life—
And dares the elements to strife!
The day is o'er;—a wide expanse
Of sky and ocean meets the glance;
And Care is at the helm to guide
The flying bark along the tide!
O happy crew! O happy bark!
To sail the sea so rough and dark,
To shun each breaker and the rock
Before you feel the horrid shock—
This—this alone should make you feel
The glow of pride in human weal,
And prompt each drooping soul to bear
Unmoved its load of human Care
And fight its battles with Despair!

III.

'Tis night;—and many a burning soul
Is drinking riot from the bowl!
And quoting many an ode to Wine
From old Anacreon—bard divine!
They'd heard Anacreon's praises sung
In many a land and many a tongue;
And now ambition to excel
In drinking long and drinking well,

Fired up the soul to sing the songs
Of ancient bards to ancient Wrongs!
Like him, they meant to quaff their wine
As if to-morrow ne'er should shine—
But should to morrow come, why then
They'd surely quaff their wine again!
And thus the crew forgot the bark,
And left her flying through the dark!
The pilot left the wheel to go
And quaff the wine cup down below,
And sing the song with wild delight—
" I will—I will be mad to-night!"
Meanwhile up blew the dread Siroc
And drove the bark athwart a rock—
Then down she went with bubbling groan,
And like a phantom ship was gone!
The Sun rose o'er the sea of Time,
But found no bark of Youth and Crime!
And days and years have rolled away,
And thousand thousands fell a prey
To Wine and to the self-same rock—
Yet many still the danger mock,
And few will shun the fatal shock!

————:0:————

THE CRUCIFIXION.

THE Sun breaks forth in splendor bright;
Before it vanishes the night!
The birds resume their notes of joy;
The awakened dead no more annoy;
The incarnate Son of God is slain,
That man might free salvation gain!
No more I'll wonder when the laws
Of Nature seem reversed, undone;
For man has now performed a crime
That shook the earth and shamed the Sun!
The sacrifice is now complete;
Salvation now for all who seek;
A God hangs lifeless on the tree,
But death shall rue the victory!

The Morning Hymn.

I.

THRICE happy he who hears Thy voice
  Bid him at earliest morn rejoice ;
'Tis as the voice of ancient Truth
To rear the energies of Youth.

II.

And Morning pours abroad the light
Around the falling throne of Night ;
Ev'n so at Thy commanding roll
Eternal truths around the soul !

III.

Thy voice is as the voice of Life ;
Thy presence quells a world of strife ;
Thy name the theme of choral song
While thousand ages roll along.

IV.

For where the power that can withstand
The Monarch-Spirit now at hand ?
Whose smile like an ethereal blaze,
Whose frown—what mortal dares to gaze ?

V.

Thou art eternal on Thy throne,
To mortal eyes the "great Unknown ;"
Yet he who seeks Thy face to know
May catch the vision ev'n below.

VI.

At morn Thy glory rises high ;
At eve Thy beauty decks the sky ;
At night Thy curtain shrouds the earth,
And loudly speaks Thy glories forth !

Is There a God?

I.

WHAT Power propels this spacious Earth of ours
Around its axis? round the blazing Sun?
What Hand directs the silent stars that run
Their daily circle round this world of ours?

II.

Who, fr m the wild abysses, called up Earth?
Who, from the depths of darkness, called up light?
Who, from the wilds of chaos, formed aright
The atmosphere and spread it round the Earth?

III.

Who gave the clouds their height? the sea its bounds?
Who gave the Earth her shape? the land its place?
Who taught the winds to run perpetual race
O'er Nature's fields that have no earthly bounds?

IV.

Who fixed the laws that formed the planets' orbs?
Who taught the Heavenly spheroids how to stray
Through trackless realms that lie athwart their way?
Who wards collision from the Heavenly orbs?

V.

Who gave the grass its color and its form?
Who taught the flower to rear its head in Spring?
Who taught the snow-cloud when and where to bring
Its crystal flakes? who gave those flakes their form?

VI.

Who taught the lightnings when to pierce the clouds?
Who taught the thunders when to shake the Sphere?
Who formed the rainbow dazzling, curved and clear,
And fixed its habitation in the clouds?

VII.

Who sends to shore the rolling tides of sea?
Who quells the wild and boisterous Ocean-storm
Which fierce advances—changes every form
Of cloud and wave—commingles sky and sea?

VIII.

Who taught the changeful Moon to hide her face
By monthly turns?   Who taught her how to pass
Through Earth's dark shadow with her cumbrous mass
Of earth-like forms, with darkness on her face?

IX.

Who quells the earthquake which upheaves the ground
And overthrows the objects of our pride?
Who gives it power through regions far and wide
To spread destruction—shake both air and ground?

X.

Who brings to naught the works of sinful man
In every age and clime?   Who brings to naught
Majestic empires?   Who to ruins brought
The Eastern World - the primal home of man?

XI.

Who taught Judea's ancient Seers to pen
Accounts of what should in the future be?
Who taught those ancient men of God to see
By faith the ripening fruit of voice and pen?

XII.

Could aught accomplish such results but God?
Can aught deny that every time and place
Abounds in further proof?   Who in the face
Of all this light can say " *There is no God!*"

XIII.

Does Atheism suppose that Chance could form
The Earth— the Heavens— and all that in them are?
Is Chance then not a God more wondrous far
Than Him we praise—more strange in life and form?

XIV.

Does Skepticism propose to live in doubts,
To see the works yet doubt the Author's power?
What cause impels at this enlightened hour
The multitude to sacrifice to doubts?

XV.

Why should I further speak?   Lives there a man
On this terrene who views the works around—
Above - to right—to left—beneath the ground—
And yet believes them formed by Chance and man?

XVI.

Whence then this god-like Man?   Might he not ask
" Whence came the God ye praise, exalt, adore?"
Can we not answer that He lived before
The Heav'ns were formed? then who need further ask?

————:o:————

THE DAY IS O'ER.

I.

THE day is o'er,
    And Night once more
Is knocking at my chamber door—
        With welcome voice
        Bids me rejoice
As in the better days of yore.

II.

    Ah, happy days!
    Fond Memory's gaze
Still pointed toward your vanished blaze,
        Mourns for the light
        Beyond the height
Where swelled the heart to notes of praise.

III.

    What now I feel
    I'll not reveal—
'Tis neither human woe nor weal—
        But crush the thought
        That Time has wrought,
As if an angel cried—"Conceal!"

IV.

    The day is o'er,
    And Night once more
Is knocking at my chamber door—
        I hear the voice
        But can't rejoice
As in the better days of yore!

The Evening Hymn.

I.

WHEN I Thy glorious works survey—
So grand by night—so grand by day—
What reverential throbbings tear
My heart, and crave an audience there!

II.

The myriad-wheeling spheres that run
Their circles round Thy dazzling throne
Hymn to the glories of Thy name,
And shout Thy praise in loud acclaim.

III.

A universal throne of fire,
Surrounded by the angelic choir,
Attends on Thy transcendent state
Whose glories Time cannot relate.

IV.

And 'mid the choir of thousand spheres
That hymn to Thee through countless years,
May I one tributary strain
Pour on the universal main?

V.

Thou art the primal source of light—
Spirit that beautifies the night—
Soul of the universe of love—
And glory of the worlds above.

VI.

And though so far above compare,
The heart that seeks Thy face in prayer
Through countless years ascending higher
Shall hymn Thy praise with tongue of fire.

The Train Ride.

I.

LET all who ride upon this car
　Think of their God—nor think in vain;
For dangerous as the sword of War
　On such a night and such a train!

II.

Yet doubtless when the danger's o'er
　The immortal soul will cease to think—
Will turn unto its haunts once more,
　When saved from Death's o'ergazing brink.

III.

Oh Christ! that man should be so frail!
　That flesh and blood should be so cheap!
That all who ride upon the rail
　Such doubtful harvest have to reap!

IV.

One moment Life is blooming high;
　The next may break the bars of Death!
For now to live and now to die
　Hang on the passing of a breath!

V.

But now 'tis o'er! The wheels are still!
　Safe—and my heart may beat once more;
Turn to the world and drink its fill,
　As often in the days of yore.

VI.

Yet should each heart upon this car
　Think of its God—nor think in vain;
For dangerous as the sword of War
　On such a night and such a train!

THE UNIVERSAL SCALES,

UPON the universal Scales I stood
    That touched the skies, and centered far below—
As deep as Hell—far o'er the wasting flood,
    In throned majesty!   The overthrow
Of nations—creeds—is 'graved upon the face
    Of this ethereal register of Truth,
In fiery letters Time cannot efface,
    Nor strong Eternity.   The voice of Youth—
Of Age—is wafted o'er the fiery flood,
    For ever 'graved upon the burning page
Of Trial!   On that fiery Scales I stood,
    Though mortal born, and of a tender age,
To weigh Jehovah's scriptures.   O'er the flood,
    Upflew the scale—the laughing-stock of Time—
And kicked the beam ;—when lo ! before me stood
    Voltaire and Hume—Gibbon with voice sublime—
Bold Ingersoll and Paine !   Repulse and shame
    Their only recompense ?—loud though their laughs,
Who stand erect upon the rocks of Fame,
    Admired by gazing fools—the walking-staffs
Of Crime and Error- -still the truthful Word
    Unshaken !   'Graved upon the eternal Page
The Truth shall stand—through ages still preferred.
    Meanwhile the voice of Wisdom and of Age
Is wafted o'er the fiery flood !   I stood
    And wept for joy upon the magic blow
On human pride ;—while o'er the wasting flood,
    Jehovah's majesty outspread below
In living splendor !   Thus I stood and gazed   .
    The universal Scales that touched the sky,
And centered far below—where Tophet blazed—
    Far o'er the flood, in throned majesty !

The Thanatopsis.

I.

THE proudest knight of Chivalry,
The serf of brutal Slavery
      Must share the lot
Assigned to man in Adam's day ;
Must mingle with his kindred clay
      And be forgot !

II.

The strongest coats of mail afford
But slight protection from the sword
      Of sterner Death
Whose empire is the spacious Earth ;
Whose subjects, all of mortal birth ;
      Whose swords, their breath !

III.

The soldier on the foughten field
With stubborn heart disdains to yield
      His cherished life,
A sacrifice to Death whose throne
Upreared on wheels of flesh and bone
      Adorns the strife.

IV.

Yet when the clouds of war have fled,
With weeping friends around his bed
      And foul disease
In every vein, he calmly waits
Till Death in mockery cries, "Too late !"
      And gives him ease !

V.

Trees have been known for years to stand
The rolling storms that whelm the land
      And Nature drown ;
Yet when no cloud was in the sky,
And not a breeze was floating by,
      To tumble down !

VI.

While others of the forest's pride
With mossy trunks that winds defied
　　And graceful form,
Have trembled in the whirling gust,
Have overturned and rolled in dust
　　Beneath the storm ;

VII.

And men have traversed sea and land
Through dangers hard to understand
　　For fame and wealth,
And when their sun was shining bright,
Been deeper plunged in darker Night
　　In bloom of health !

VIII.

On every breeze that passes by
Death rides a sovereign throned on high ;
　　And in the storm
Distinctly are his traces seen,
For there his wheels he sits between
　　In hideous form !

IX.

Where'er the germs of Life are seen,
The seeds of Death are found between
　　Their vital parts ;
And where Disease is dreaded least,
Grim Death ordains a royal feast
　　And Life departs !

X.

What has the flight of ages taught?
To what a scene of ruin brought
　　The Eastern World ?
How fares it with the States of Earth,
E'en those conspicuous most for worth,
　　When Death is hurled ?

XI.

E'en as the whirlwind's rolling car
Spreads devastation wide and far
　　Amid the heath,
So empires with their flags unfurled
Are from their ancient centers hurled
　　By sterner Death !

XII.

Seek not eternal life on Earth
Where all took either rise or birth
    Predoomed to die;
For all that have not paid the debt
Must fill the dreadful summons yet,
    Must fall and lie!

——:o:——

THE MUSICIAN.

I.

SHOW me the man of music full,
  Of jollity and smiling;
His are my joys—his ease my rest—
  The sullen hours beguiling.

II.

Yes, bring him forth—he is my friend—
  No matter what his name is,
His station, wealth and ancestry;
  To me it all the same is.

III.

But hide, oh! hide from me the face
  Where music ne'er hath risen;
With such in view—where'er the place—
  To me 'twere but a prison.

IV.

Let such alone; molest them not;
  Their gloom let still surround them;
Let them bewail their bitter lot
  And tighter strap it round them!

THE MIDNIGHT HYMN.

I.

THY temple is the endless space
　Where burning suns attend the chase;
And in this temple of the skies
What clouds of holy incense rise!

II.

Around Thee all the skies are furled
In peerless grandeur o'er the world;
And rolling stars aspire to own
The wheels of Thy eternal throne.

III.

Far in the long forgotten Past
Thy Spirit rode throughout the vast,
And bade the wilds of chaos own
The star wheel of the Eternal's throne!

IV.

And life and order sprung sublime
To note the glorious birth of Time;
And darkness fled the realm of Night
At Thy command, " Let there be light!"

V.

How vain the petty works of man
Compared to Thy eternal plan!
To Thee all Nature's works belong
That hymn Thy name in choral song.

VI.

From everlasting Thou art grand!
To everlasting Thou shalt stand!
And all who live and all who die
Shall hail Thee monarch of the sky!

THE VOICES OF THE NIGHT.

I.

WELL might the swart Chaldean raise
   Aloft his wondering eyes—
Ev'n in those dark barbaric days—
   To gaze upon the skies.
Why not?—for Art had never spread
   Her glories o'er the waiting earth ;
Where'er the gazer turned to tread
   Strong Nature stood, the source of worth ;
But most by night her glories shine,
And nearer bring the border-line
To mortal view, where intertwine
The living glories here below
   With living glories far above,
And all with light and life aglow,
   And all the charms and powers of love.

II.

Hark to the voice of Night—
It falls upon the ear
In melodies so clear !
And he who lists may hear
The tolling knell of Time's
Disasters, woes and crimes.
The temple of the sky
   Stands forth, a vasty dome
Upreared and curtained high,
   And calls me forth to roam ;
And every star its place hath found,
From whence to scatter light around ;
Hark to the happy, happy sound,
   As Nature's train goes by—
   The voices of the sky !

III.

So sweet the enchanting melody—
   What voice could imitate?
So perfect is the harmony—
   When known to mortal state?

The bloody lessons of the Past
In one dark reservoir we cast,
  Whene'er we hear aright,
In universal harmony,
  The voices of the Night.

IV.

Light cries aloud, " At work am I!"
For proof the myriad stars rush by :
There Darkness cries, " No foe am I!"
For proof he seems to kiss the sky :
There Order cries, "To duty I!"
For proof behold the harmony :
There Love still whispers, "Sick am I!"
Whose heart can not thus testify ?

V.

Down with the everlasting jar
Of mortals rushing on to war!
Down with the powers of bated Hate!
Down with the tyrant, small or great!
Down with the gyves—though silver-bright—
That shackle the approach of Light!
Let man, as in the days of yore,
  Seek hidden light beneath the stars,
Until his heart's most inmost core
  . Attests the magic spell,
    And cries aloud, " How well!"

VI.

Long had I sought to know the truth ;
  I found it where I least had thought ;
The woe that gilds the fall of Youth
  Contains the oracle I sought :
So at the overthrow of Day,
  A thousand lights adorn the skies,
  And pour their light on mortal eyes,
And banish gloomy thoughts away,
Which else had held supreme control,
And terrorized the human soul.

VII.

That which is done is done through time ;
  Not gods the law could change!
The good is good—the crime is crime—
Whoever think it strange ;

The voice of Love, when heard aright,
Re echoes sweetly through the night,
　While o'er the vision far,
　　The starry worlds above
　Forget chaotic war
　　And only think of love!
Thus by the first of Nature's laws—
The law of stern effect and cause—
　Where Love once sets his seal
　　He stamps eternal doom
　Of misery or weal
　　Through all the time to come.
What marvel then if man
Adore the wondrous Plan
That never shows aright
Except at deepest night?

VIII.

For fallen love there is a balm;
　Behold it in the skies!
The tempest fades into a calm,—
　The world, to paradise!
Hail then the voices of the sky,
　That speak to man such living truth!
Though Love may fall, and Hope may die,
　And all the energies of Youth,
Still in the skies the sign is spread
　Of order, truth and love,
The flaming sign of happiness
　Far in the worlds above.

IX.

Hail to the voice of Love at night!
All hail to Order's voice at Night!
All hail to Light's faint voice at night!
Hail to the voice of Night at night!
The world is beautiful around;
　The skies are beautiful above;
A thousand voices strike the sound,
　And every voice is filled with love!

X.

Well might the swart Chaldean raise
　Aloft his wondering eyes—

Ev'n in those dark barbaric days—
  To gaze upon the skies.
Why not?--for Art had never spread
  Her glories o'er the waiting earth ;
Where'er the gazer turned to tread
  Strong Nature stood, the source of worth ;
But most by night her glories shine,
And nearer bring the border line
To mortal view, where intertwine
The living glories here below
  With living glories far above ;
And all with light and life aglow,
  And all the charms and powers of love.

————:o:————

THE DRUNKARD'S WIFE.

I.

THE night was gloomy—dark—and cold,
  And from the eastern sky no light ;
Each maddening blast new horrors told
  Attendant on the gusty night.

II.

The fire was dead, and o'er its tomb
  Of ashes, wrapped in sorrow sore,
A worse than widowed mother whom
  The pitchy night no salace bore.

III.

She will not yet embrace Despair—
  She still has hoping of relief ;
She will not tear her lovely hair,
  Nor wholly give away to grief.

IV.

She mourns—her husband's loss of pride ;
  She feels—yet almost doubts the truth ;
'Tis done ;—she can no more confide
  In him who loved her so in youth !

V.

The drunkard still remains away;
  The babe and mother colder grow;
The infant sleeps;—a glimmering ray
  Of light unclouds her glimmering brow—

VI.

She hears him coming? O what joy!
  'Tis past!—'twas but the rustling leaves—
And she alone! dark Nights annoy,
  A troubled web of sorrow weaves.

VII.

The infant sleeps—the sleep of death!
  The mother lies upon the floor,
And sighs in vain with every breath
  For whom she did at first adore!

VIII.

No more she rates him "drunken brute"—
  Love will a thousand faults forget—
She now recalls her dreamy youth
  When Love's eternal beauty set!

IX.

Still howl the winds around the door;
  Time ushers on the dead of night;
The youthful mother sorrows sore,
  And waits impatient for the light—

X.

The drunkard came at last, and called;
  No voice replied; he burst the door
To find the hand of Death had wrought
  Sad havoc on his cabin floor!

THE HANDWRITING ON THE WALL.

BELSHAZZAR reigned in Babylon, and his throne
　Was paramount in all the nations known ;
And dwelling in his royal palace halls,
Begirt with Babylon's broad and massy walls,
He felt secure from danger and alarms,
Feared no assaulting shock of men-at-arms.
His predecessors on the Imperial throne
Had made Chaldea's iron scepter known
In many a distant land and region old
From whence his tribute flowed of slaves and gold.
And now Belshazzar proclamation made
That all his nobles, sumptuously arrayed,
Should with himself, his wives and concubines
Unite and feast upon his choicest wines.
Both courtiers gay and satraps heard the call
And straight repaired to King Belshazzar's hall :
The king was present in his robe of State ;
The banquet hall was thronged from throne to gate ;
And many a brilliant lamp of ancient mould
Shone from its chandelier of burnished gold ;
And many a noble of that doomed land
Was drinking riot at the king's command ;
When lo ! a hand of wildering aspect bright,
Appeared, and on the wall began to write !
Few were the words those angel fingers wrote,
But each sang audibly a funeral note ;
Few were the letters by those fingers traced,
But each appeared with tenfold horror graced ;
And now his charge performed—the warning given—
The angel reascended into Heaven ;
Yet still those words of unknown meaning shone
From off the palace wall beside the throne !
As, when of old, their sires attempted vain
To build a tower to Heaven from Shinar's plain,
Jehovah from above descending down
To view the tower, the builders and the town,
Confused their language to so dread extent
That each knew naught of what another's meant—

With one accord they left the tower alone,
Awed by the presence of the great Unknown:
So from Belshazzar's feast the frightened guests
No longer mindful of their king's behests,
Each as his fancy led—both great and small—
Turned in contempt. or left the haunted hall.
Belshazzar gave command: "Chaldea's seers,
Rise and expound what in these words appears
Mysterious!" Advancing at his call,
They view the dread handwriting on the wall:
"These words by us were never seen before!"
Thus virtually—"We see but know no more!"
And when these masters of Chaldean lore
Had viewed the wondrous letters o'er and o'er,
And failed to note e'en one expressive word,
The mild assurance of the queen was heard:
"Let Daniel come, the Captive; he can best
Expound these words that mar our royal rest,
For in him dwell the spirits of the God!"
To whom the king replied, "Perhaps he can!"
Then turning to the guards—"Bring forth the man!"
Then all were silent save those words unknown
That shone from off the wall beside the throne.
When Daniel entered that illumined hall,
He gazed the dread handwriting on the wall,
And then to King Belshazzar: "Though thy sire,
Nebuchadnezzar, felt Jehovah's ire,
For proud persistence in his wicked ways,
When with the cattle he was glad to graze;
And though thou knew'st the story of his fate—
Thou, the inheritor of his throne and State,
Hast followed in his footsteps till the hand
Of great Jehovah, armed against thy land,
Hath broke the Babylonian's power in twain,
As tempests dash rude vessels on the main!"
Then turning to the letters on the wall:
"*Mene, mene, tekel upharsin!* All
Related curses for thyself and throne:
*Belshazzar's grave is made; his kingdom gone;
The Mede and Persian occupy his throne!*"
That night the king was slain; and on the morn,
With joyous shout and peal of trumpet-horn,
Darius entered through the Royal Gate,
And took possession of the throne of State.

Apostrophe to the Sun.

CENTER of life and light ! though art the source
   Of boundless power.   Thou art a sovereign throned
Of all the land, all the boundless sea,
Whose title none dispute.   In earlier times,
Ere man's aspiring mind attained to thoughts
Of nobler Essence, ere the Eternal Word
That framed thy mighty bulk and fired it up,
Had deigned to guide his mind, immortal man,
In adoration viewed thy flaming face
And called it God ! and e'en till now, O Sun
Thou'rt held in awe and reckoned 'mong the gods
In various lands !   But we who sing thy praise
This evening, hold thee not among the gods,
But as the mightiest bulk of workmanship
Which God in wisdom placed in view of Earth
To teach his power.   With inspiration full
Thou art and power to soothe ; and shalt remain
Through ceaseless time.   Thou rollest fiercely on
Forever, 'thwart the broad cerulean dome,
Yet changest not nor tirest.   Each fleeting day,
Thou climbst the sky, and viewest this nether world,
And shootst abroad thy rays of seven-fold light
Down through the trackless void, and fallst toward Earth,
And sinkst beneath the horizon's circling girt,
And hidest from view ; and while for us 'tis night,
Thou wheelst thy fiery car and rollest back—
By us unseen—and reappearest at morn.
O inexhaustible store of wealth and life !
O priceless jewell in our firmament set
By wise Omnipotence !   From forth thy face,
In emanations swift through Heaven's expanse,
Thy light and heat advance.   Thou risest high,
And bringst the Summer forth, and givest the Earth
Her flowery robe, and causest fruit to grow
And every herb, and wakest the lightnings up,
That rend the furious clouds aloft in air
Throned on the rolling winds.   Thou rollest back :—

Dread Winter takes his stand ; the hills are bare ;
The thunders cease to fling their fiery bolts ;
And but for thy return, all Earth were void
And life would cease.   Sublime and dreadful sphere!
Thou rolling ball, thou world of moving fire !
Whence all thy power so like Omnipotence?
Who taught thee how to drive thy furious car
O'er Heaven's cerulean dome?   Who lit the flames
That wrap thy face with fire and shoot their beams
Of living heat throughout thy vast domain ?
Who strewed the worlds around thy burning throne,
And gave thee power to hurl them round thyself
Till worlds shall end?   Who gave thee power to rule
The surging tides of Ocean's boundless depths?
What Power prevents thy ceaseless burning mass
From falling into naught, by flames devoured?
Who cleareth from out thy way the Heavenly orbs
That thou full scope might have to rush thy car
Still headlong on with flames and smoke inwrapped ?
"God! God!" shine forth the hills that rear their heads
To catch thy dawning smile, thy parting glimpse ;
"God!" shout the clouds that ceaseless ride the air
In furious storms; the winds shriek loudly, " God !"
The lightnings rush from out their secret hide,
And loudly burst the echoing thunder tones
That shake both Earth and Heaven and cry out, " God !"
And now thou shootst thy beams amid the storm,
And sets in every cloud thy radiant bow
That strides the air and whispers softly, " God !"
And far beyond the Equatorial girt
Where lies the Earth with ice and snow enrobed,
Both land and Ocean ceaseless utter " God !"
And e'en the Earth, the stars, the Heavens themselves,
Still onward fly and catch the echo, " God !"
Whilst thou, O Sun! who hast thy dazzling throne
Both night and day—with thee there is no night—
High up in Heaven among thy kindred spheres,
Still rollest on—both round thy flaming self
And round the central Universal Throne—
And lookst abroad throughout thy bright domain
Lit by the flaming rays received from God,
And cryest aloud and ceaseless, " God is Power !"

THE OVERTHROW OF BABYLON.

I.

BELSHAZZAR sat upon his throne,
A sovereign proud in Babylon ;
Before him sat at festal boards
    A thousand lords.

II.

The king commanded every knee
To bow in deap humility,
To gods of wood, and brass, and stone ;
    The feat was done!

III.

His guests arose : upon the wall
A hand appeared ; and over all
A terror spread as if to note
    The words it wrote !

IV.

The graven letters stood unknown
Upon the wall beside the throne
Till Daniel came—the captive Jew—
    And ran them through.

V.

He read : " Belshazzar's grave is made,
His kingdom gone !   His power is weighed !
His throne the Persian and the Mede
    Usurp with speed !"

VI.

That night the king was slain ; and when
The morning woke to life again,
Darius climbed the throne of State
    And sealed its fate.

THE SON OF ABOU KHAN.

I.

THERE lived a knight of Hindoostan,
    A worthy son of Abou Khan,
Who bred and born to Buddhist views
Still held a preterence for the Jews.
He read of Shadrach's fiery bed,
And how the angel sentries stood,
Of Daniel in the lion's den,
And how he stood there unsubdued ;
Elijah and Elisha too
Before him passed in strict review—
And David with his slinging-stone
To fight Goliath all alone—
These stories in his youth he heard,
Believing firmly every word !
So when he paused upon the brink
Of sterner manhood, there to think
Awhile upon the various roads
By greater and by lesser Gods
Chalked out on earth for human life,
This worthy son of Abou Khan,
A valiant knight of Hindoostan,
Renounced at once his father's creed,
Became a Jew in word and deed,
And cried to all who round him trod—
" Jehovah is the only God !"

II.

And time rolled on—and on—yet still
He worshipped toward Moria's hill !
He was a Jew in deed and word,
Believed their Scriptures every word,
Yet living in a land unknown
To Jewish or to Western throne !
Ev'n Alexander failed to pass
    The streamlet where his cottage stood !
Around him dwelt in solid mass
    The Buddhist votaries unsubdued ;

And when their laws were pointed forth
He shouted to the sons of earth—
" I'll worship as my heart inspires,
Though doomed thereby to penal fires !"
And thus he held his creed—his name—
As if his country held the same ;
Unmindful of the savage thirst
Of church fanatics, far the worst
That ever entered court to swear
Against the doomed to despair !

III.

A year rolled on ;—and Abou Khan,
A shining light of Hindoostan,
Was childless 'cause his son had trod
The footsteps of a foreign God !
Religion ! in thy godly name
    What godless crimes do men commit !
Crimes that would bring the Devil to shame
    Cast on the gods of holiest Writ !
Let others serve the God they choose,
The Islam's—Buddhist's—or the Jew's ;
For me, I'll take the dangerous plan,
Like this lone star of Hindoostan,
And worship as my heart inspires,
Though doomed thereby to penal fires !
For since the light began to glow,
And man began the truth to know,
No greater crime hath marked the world,
Or o'er the human race been hurled,
Than his who with his neighbor strives
To fasten Conscience in the gyves !
For Conscience still will break, and soar,
Believing all it did before,
Though monarchs frown and tyrants rave
And turn the garden to a grave !

The Midnight Lamp.

I.

'TWAS not the workman's tool alone
   That gave the earth her living stamp;
'Twas aided by the " great Unknown,"
   And by the blazing Midnight lamp.

II.

The voice of Nature sounds serene
   Where Midnight sets her sacred stamp;
The throne of Worth is ever seen
   Where burns the blazing Midnight lamp.

III.

The blazing of the Midday Sun
   Sufficeth for the woodman's tramp;
But Wisdom hovers round her throne
   Where burns the blazing Midnight lamp.

IV.

What is the genius of our age?
   What gave us our progressive stamp?
What brightens our historic page?—
   The energetic Midnight lamp.

V.

The voice of Nature cries aloud
   Where Midnight sets her sacred stamp;
Yea, speaks as though a fiery cloud
   That hovers round the Midnight lamp.

The Song at the Red Sea.

JEHOVAH is a man of war! Jehovah let us sing!
Jehovah is the God of peace—the universal King!
The chariot and the charioteer to Him as naught appear;
He breathes upon the mailed ranks—and thousands disap-
     pear!
The horses and the riders lie beneath the angry flood,
The battle-flag forever furled, and hushed the cry of blood!
The servitude of Israel in a foreign land is o'er!
The Slave is now emancipate and on a distant shore!
The lofty pyramids beside the lordly Nile may stand,
To teach the future ages where the Pharaohs held command,
Yet still the name of Egypt fails through all the time to
     come;
Such is Jehovah's living curse—and such is Egypt's doom!
The Egyptian monarchies a proud and triple pillar stood,
Though oft assailed by Time and War, as often unsubdued,
Until their kings perfected all the heinous arts of Crime,
Then fell in horrid overthrow—the laughing-stock of Time!
Yet not alone is Pharaoh's haughty State the seat of crimes,
The blazing sentinels of Ruin to the future times;
The voice of Love is silent through the wild and broad ex-
     panse—
Why seek for love where man adores the hated sword and
     lance?
And Science, yet unborn, hears wild and undisturbed rage,
And leaps in vain to catch the light—each hour a sunless
     age—
Till through the boundless Orient a living voice is heard,
And new-born Science springs to life, and speaks the magic
     word
That disenthrones a thousand gods, and pours the living light
Of Truth around the boasted throne of old and boastful
     Night!
Then let the voice of Hope abound along the rugged shore,
Till mountain-crag to mountain-crag repeat our triumphs o'er!
And cry, "Jehovah's warrior might—Jehovah's praise we
     sing!
The everlasting God of peace—the universal King!"

After the Storm

HOW brilliant 'twixt the ritted clouds appears
The orient Sun, as o'er the mountain's crest
He rears his head to bid the tempest rest!
All night the winds around the fixed spheres
Howled in terrific fury, giving Night
A double terror; while the heart of man
In deep emotion tried in vain to scan
The depth of Nature in her far delight.
Hail then the dawning of another Day
That o'er the realm of Tempest and of Night
Re rears the standard and the power of Light,
And scatters brilliance through the rising spray!
Hail radiant Sun! Thy kind return inspires
The weary heart that had despaired of life,
To pluck fresh courage for each coming strife.
E'en as the earth beneath thy kindling fires
Puts on her verdurous robe of Nature's green
And blooms and shakes and o'er the tomb of Death
Spreads shrouds of living green, fanned by the breath
Of spicy gales that o'er the freshening scene
Serenely float and charm the passer by:
Ev'n so when o'er the ruined wrecks of Fame
The sun of Hope arises to reclaim
Our primal state of life and purity!
Such is the awful mystery of life!
When dread Disaster with monarchic stride
O'erturns our confidence and scorns our pride,
Life plucks fresh vigor from the rolling strife,
And springs erelong from out the wrecks of Time
More vivid than before and more sublime!

PART SIXTH.

THE TWO SONGS.

I.

NOW let the freemen sing the song
    Of Right throughout the lands of Wrong!
And every mountain wake to hear
The anthem martyrs held so dear!
And every breeze forget to blow;
And every brook forget to flow;
And every soul prolong the strain
That swells from mountain-top to main,
Preserving in its verse sublime
The grandest memories of Time
And giving many an honored name
To future ages and to Fame!
Yea, strike the song from shore to shore
Till tyrants' thrones shall be no more!
And every martyr's tears be dried
Through lands of freedom far and wide!
Till all shall join—a happy train—
To sing in many an ancient strain
Reflected from an age of night,
The song of Wrong in lands of Right!

II.

The freemen heard those words of fire;
Then struck the loud resounding lyre!
They chanted loud—they chanted long—
Throughout the dismal lands of Wrong!
They sung by night—they sung by day—
   They sung by land—they sung by sea—
They sung where monarchs held their sway—
   They sung where every glen is free—
They sung till traitors fled the sight,
The mighty song of mighty Right!

III.

Still let the joyous strains prolong;
Let pealing organs peal the song!
Till every mountain wakes to hear
The anthem martyrs held so dear!
And every breeze forgets to blow;
And every brook forgets to flow;
And every soul prolongs the strain
That swells from mountain-top to main,
And tells of freedom's battles won
Through all the circuit of the sun!
For every liberty we own
Was wrested from a tyrant's throne;
And every flower that scents the morn
Was gathered from a spiry thorn!

IV.

But tyrants' thrones are now no more
On eastern or on western shore;
And all shall join—a happy train—
To sing in many an ancient strain
The praise of those who sung in vain
And cried from mountain-top to main,
In spite of scorn, in spite of pain,
Their present loss—but future gain—
Yea all shall sing with wild delight
At home—abroad—by day—by night—
The song of Wrong in lands of Right!

THE TRIAL BY JURY.

I.

OF all the great bulwarks set up for the free
   By the blood of the martyrs—the wisdom of sages—
The trial by Jury—who would not agree?—
   Stands forth as the brightest bequest of the ages.

II.

The trial by Jury! where first it appeared,
   We know not nor care ;—but we hail it with song
As the grandest tribunal that ever was reared
   To establish the right and prohibit the wrong—

III.

The pillar of Freedom—the engine of Truth—
   The rock of Defense—the great structure of ages :—
It grappled with Tyranny even in youth—
   And came off a victor applauded by sages.

IV.

And even the tyrant of Normandy's shore
   Who thrived on the ruins of England—ev'n he,
Though he trod Saxon liberties down by the score,
   Found the Jury a bulwark reserved to the free.

V.

And the warrior with thousands of men at his heels
   And millions of money—which Freedom so loathes—
Is put to the rout when the country once feels
   The power of twelve honest men armed with their oaths!

Bunker's Hill.[1]

I.

ARISE, imperial Bunker! shake
  Thy firmest set foundation stone!
Bid anarchs, kings and tyrants quake,
  . And bury in Oblivion
  The memory of Oppression's throne!

II.

Thy hill so calm to present gaze
  Was once the seat of roaring War;
Thy sheeted crest with fire ablaze
  Shot deadly missiles near and far
  Revolving like a falling star!

III.

Here fell the patriots' blood as rain,
  Spilt in defense of Freedom's cause;
Here bristling steel and leaden hail
  Strove 'gainst each other scorning pause,
  Those for, these 'gainst King George's laws.

IV.

Immortal Warren! o'er thy bones
  Let Freedom weep a double tear—
Half in defiance of the thrones,
  And half lamenting that the bier
  Should be employed so proudly here!

V.

And yet methinks on Bunker's Hill
  Were grandest tomb to mortals known;
Yea kings their glory to fulfill
  Would quit the terror-haunted throne
  To sleep on Bunkner's crest alone!

VI.

Freedom! immortal Bunker's name
  Be guarded by thy holiest ties!
Let the eternal trump of Fame

Re echo through the Western skies,
Till Bunker's proudest memories rise!

VI.

Spirit of Bunker! deign to fill
The sons of sires who won renown
Upon thy world-applauded hill—
And oh! forbid the tempting crown
To tear thy ancient glories down!

————:o:—-—

IN THE ALLEGHANIES.

NO tyrant here can wield the cursed rod
Where all breathe free the atmosphere of God!
This goodly land by Nature's stern decree
Was pre-ordained a land of liberty.
Witness ye mountains whose eternal crests
O'ergaze the landscape where the brooklet rests;
Witness ye crystal brooks that flow serene
The rough and jagged mountain-ribs between;
Or witness all ye hardy sons of men
Who rule as monarchs of the peaceful glen,
Where every breeze that passes softly by
Kisses the trees and whispers, "Liberty!"
O earth! where such another land as this?
Where such a dearth of woe? such stores of bliss?
Pure crystal brooklets flow the hills between;
High monarch mountains clothe the verdurous scene;
While vasty torrents rushing heedless by
O'er precipices joining earth and sky,
Co-rival in their fierce and far delight
Yosemite's or steep Niagara's might!

THE ORACLE.

I.

YEARS on years—and age on ages—
Roll along the fields of Glory,
Filling all historic pages
With the cry of prisoned debtors
And the clang of Whig and Tory;—
But the sons of toil and labor
Reap no harvest from the saber;
And the endless jar and jargon
Hide the causes of the story.

II.

What is Greece?   A servile nation,
Racked and torn by local fetters—
Tomb of far historic Ages—
Temple of the gods and sages—
In the midst of hostile nations,
All surrounded:—once her station
Ranked the first, the grandest nation
Known to mortals!   In her Athens,
Socrates aspired to' glory—
Gave his creed to waiting nations—
Died,—and ended up the story;
Pericles—and Alexander—
Stern Demo-thenes—ah, Glory!
Vainly do we read thy story,
Graven on historic pages—
Greece is gone, and half forgotten
By the wise—the modern sages!
Glory is a torch that flickers
O'er the outer sea of darkness,
Flickers now, and brighter blazes- -
Lures the wisest through its mazes—
Dies,—and leaves us to its phases!

III.

What has France to claim the vision?
On we hie to lands Elysian!
To the land of warlike Saxons—

Boasted land of boasted Freedom,
Both a farce! The love of glory—
Still the burden of their story—
Glory through succeeding ages—
Glory in the pangs of Freedom
'Graven on historic pages!
Witness Europe! witness Asia!
Africa and proud Columbia!
Last and greatest, witness Ireland!
Land of debtors!—land of labor!—
Tyrants' home!—and grave of Freedom!
Land where he who lifts the saber
Dies the death! The immortal story,
Writ in blood but not in glory,
One eternal beacon 'blazes—
Meets the eye where'er it gazes—
Calls for man's enduring praises.

IV.

Seven hundred years of labor—
Foreign lords have held the harvest!
Often rising with the saber—
Still her faith remains unshaken;—
Jews and Greeks have fought for ages,
Fought and bled in quest of Freedom—
But the Irish faith surpasses
Aught upon historic pages;
Irishmen have wept for ages—
Fought for freedom through all stages—
Fought for all, but got no wages—
Wept and died in foreign cages—
Plied the storm where'er it rages—
Gave the English tongue her sages —
Eat the bread of toil in sorrow—
Still have hoping for the morrow!
Still have hope to see the Saxon
Banished from this isle of sorrow!
Still have hope of Ireland's banners
Waving o'er her ancient people!
Still have hope to hear the shouts of
Freedom from each tower and steeple!
Still have hope—their foes all smitten—
Hope to see the hope of ages—
Emmet's epitaph be written!

In Futuro.

I.

A SPIRIT hovers o'er the East
  The future seat of roaring war,
Where flapping vultures soon shall feast
  On armies hailing from afar.

II.

Woe to the empire of the Turk,
  That soon shall pass to bloodier hands!
'Tis Time's decree; but bloody work
  Must first o'erthrow those classic lands!

III.

Ah! wrapped with fires of future wars,
  Full many a Scio 'gins to blaze;
And groaning 'neath the lash of Mars,
  From shore to shore the nations gaze.

IV.

From Ethiope to the Azof Sea
  The fires extend; while sounds the shock
Of tyrants warring with the free
  From Ganges to Gibraltar's rock.

V.

Wildly the tide of blood and tears
  Pours o'er the century-trodden East;
And louder than for thousand years,
  Death grins in mockery at the feast.

VI.

But lo! the Turk for Tartar plains
  Departs to take his ancient stand!
No longer stern Mahomet reigns!
  But other tyrants spoil the land!

THE WHIPPING POST TREE.

I.

THE walnut of Fishkill still stands as a mark
   Of the barbarous practice upheld by our sires ;
But Nature has wrapped in her mantle of bark
   The engine the tyrant so greatly admires!

II.

Here stood the scared Tory fast chained to the tree ;
   By his side the deserter from Amric's wars!
And the merciless cowhide—that scourge of the free—
   Was brought forth—a disgrace to the calling of Mars!

III.

And this was for freedom?—aye, freedom indeed!
   Such freedom as Jefferson never defended!
Ah no! 'twas camp-followers did the foul deed.
   Whose names should no longer with freedom's be blended!

IV.

And now what remains for the poet to sing?
   The fame of the scoundrel is blent with the sage's!
And the cause of the hero who hated his king
   Is disgraced by the barbarous practice of ages!

V.

And shall I then sing of the conquests sublime
   Of the cause of the free—gaining strength with each age—
Unawed by the villainies grafted on crime
   'Neath the banner of freedom—the cause of the sage?

VI.

Shall I sing of the glories of Washington's zeal—
   Of Jefferson's fire—and of Hamilton's skill—
Of Adams—and Henry—and yet never feel
   The blushing of shame for the tree of Fishkill?

VII.

The blushing of shame on a sea of wild pride
   Pours a gloom o'er the Present, a cloud o'er the Past ;
But it works for the Future what years have denied—
   A freedom unbounded—a boon which shall last!

VIII.

Then let the lou l clarion sound through the land
  Till the fame of our freedom fills valley and hill ;
And the chivalrous deeds of our sages shall brand
  With darkest Oblivion the tree of Fishkill!

————:o:————

Arnold's March to Canada,

I.

BEHOLD from out the Wilderness
  This gallant band emerging forth,
Sworn to avenge their late distress
And carry war into the North !
How valiant beats each manly heart !
How glows the cheek at sight of art !
For art of man by them unseen
Throughout the dreary march hath been !

II.

They marshal round their standard, and ·
A formidable front present
To all the dread monarchic bands
Of widespread Canada's extent ;
Unfurled their standards flaunt the sky
And urge to deeds of victory ;
The future Traitor sounds the alarms
And all his warriors stand in arms !

III.

O that the soul of him that leads
This valiant band of warriors forth
Had firmness to resist the greed
That lures the wisest sons of Earth !
But this is not ; nor can we tell
What cause inspires the brave to sell ;
But this we see from times afar—
The greatest criminal is War !

THE SURRENDER OF CORNWALLIS.

I.

'TIS done ;—the martial drum no more
  Shall rouse Columbia's sons to arms ;
  The cloud of war is gone ; the roar
  Re-echoes not in wild alarms ;
Eternal Freedom ceaseless be adored—
Cornwallis tenders now his hostile sword !

II.

  Heroic hearts that dared to brave
  War's thunders rolling fierce and high,
  That scorned the terror of the wave—
  Resolved with liberty to die
Or live with Victory—War's destruction poured
In furious streams that gained Cornwallis' sword !

III.

  Brave hearts that wept when from the North
  War's thundering echoes first were heard,
  Heroic souls that marshalled forth
  To bloodiest war without a word,
Rejoice ! for Victory leaves the English Lord !
Cornwallis now presents his hostile sword !

IV.

  Throughout the States let music roll ;
  Let joy resume her ancient stand ;
  Let liberty assume control,
  A sovereign of this glorious land :
Peace ! stand in triumph where the War has roared !
For now Cornwallis tenders George his sword !

V.

  Time ! hast thou seen a worthier sight ?
  Freedom ! thy reign is now secure !
  Earth ! hail the breaking up of Night !
  Columbia ! hold thy victory sure !
And every freeman praise the living Lord !
For now Cornwallis yields his hostile sword !

GRANDFATHER'S CLOCK.

I.

ENTHRONED upon thy ancient mantel-tree
O king of clocks! thou 'rt ever dear to me,
As with a tireless stroke that scorns at rest,
   Thy ticks and tocks—
   O king of clocks!—
Cry out aloud to all, " To work is best!"

II.

Thou first of clocks that ever told the time
In grand old Logan! o'er thy throne sublime
Have more than fifty arm-d winters rolled
   And yet thy tocks—
   O king of clocks!—
Are clear and sweet as in the days of old.

III.

Immortal fame to Terry and his son,
Thy valor gives, as standing on thy throne
Thou mak'st thy impress on the sands of Time ;
   Thy ticks and tocks—
   O king of clocks!—
Preserve their names and make thy throne sublime.

IV.

Let others share thy master's hidden gold
When he shall sleep in Death's eternal fold.
If I survive I'll only ask for thee!
   Thy ticks and tocks—
   O king of clocks!—
Were legacy and wealth enough for me!

V.

Since first thy race began, one race of men
Has lived—and died—and turned to dust again ;
And yet thou seem'st in vigor's prime of youth!
   Thy ticks and tocks—
   O king of clocks!—
Are like the workings of eternal Truth.

VI.

Grim War hath swept around thy peaceful throne,
And hurled into the land of the unknown
Some of thy household resting now afar ;
     And yet thy tocks—
     O king of clocks !—
Did never halt to curse the murderous War.

VII.

And now of late thou art again bereft,
Another faithful friend ! yea, thou art left
To unskilled hands that on thy wants attend ;
     And yet thy tocks—
     O king of clocks !—
Gave but a single day to mourn her end !

VIII.

Thou first and last of clocks ! when thou art done
Thy mortal race, and standest on thy throne
A lifeless thing, my tears thy fall shall weep ;
     For with thy tocks—
     O king of clocks !- -
So often hast thou rocked my youth to sleep !

———:o:———

THE JEW'S LAMENT.

I.

FOREVER must I vainly weep
   O'er Salem's fall and I-rael's loss?
Salem ! arise from out thy sleep—
   Refine thy gold and burn thy dross.

II.

The voice of music once did float
   In sweetness o'er thy hills serene ;
But now how different sounds the note
   That rolls thy ruined walls between !

III.

The wisest king of ancient days
  In thee upreared his throne of State;
Now from thy hills the unlettered gaze
  Of *slaves*—such is the tyranny of Fate!

IV.

Yea! in thy ancient Temple deigned
  Jehovah to descend in light!
But stranger gods have long profaned
  Thy hills through many an age of night.

V.

And twice a thousand circling years
  Have failed to cure thy cureless woe,
And scorned the sacrifice of tears
  Shed o'er thy ruinous overthrow.

VI.

In thee no more loud shouts are heard,
  As erst in days more truly blest,
At promulgation of the Word
  Revealed on Sinai's thundering crest;

VII.

For lo! a Mosque upreared on high!
  What profanation of the Truth!
And yet 'tis vain to heave the sigh,
  Or mourn the overthrow of Youth.

VIII.

Why slumbers thus the sword of Death?
  Deserves no other State the stroke?
Shall Israel dwell upon the heath
  Forever 'neath the tyrant's yoke?

IX.

And will Jehovah never smile
  On lands where once Shechinah dwelt?
Shall Israel mourn while foes the while
  Boast o'er the ruin they have dealt?

X.

And must I weep forever more
  O'er Salem's fall and Israel's loss?
Rise, Salem! to the race once more!
  Refine thy gold and burn thy dross!

THE LAND OF OUR FATHERS.

I.

THE land of our fathers is holiest ground;
  There their blood in defense of our freedom they spilt;
And curst be the tyrant who lingers around
  To destroy the proud temple our forefathers built!

II.

The voice of a century cries to the world
  In behalf of our freedom so hallowed in song;
And we march to the conquest with banners unfurled,
  Singing songs of the Right in the lands of the Wrong.

III.

And history now opes a new page of her book—
  A page to record the successes of Peace!
And the poet now sings without fear of rebuke
  The shame of the warrior—whose glories now cease!

IV.

Strike a blow at our freedom?—the world is undone!
  We are here from the uttermost parts of the earth!
For the pilgrims from Zembla to lands of the Sun
  Struck tent when they heard of our Union's proud birth!

V.

The Irishman's love of his country prevails
  When the heat of debate stirs the depths o the soul;
And the might of the Saxon is seen when the gales
  Threaten wreck to our vessels in search of the Pole!

VI.

The German is here in his love for the vine;
  The Frank in his freedom untrammeled by creed;
The Switzer may here find a lovelier Rhine,
  And a new race of Tells to adorn— not to bleed!

VII.

O land of the stranger! O home of the free!
  May thy glories increase on the pages of Time!
And thy freedom a marvel, a watchword shall be
  To the warriors of Truth in each country of Crime!

VIII.

And the voice of the ages shall shout to the world
  The worth of our freedom so hallowed in song;
While we march to the conquest wiih banners unfurled,
  Singing songs of the Right in the lands of the Wrong!

PART SEVENTH.

THE POWER OF FRIGHT.

I.

A TRAVELER met at Cairo's gate
A monster clad in regal state;
The Eastern Plague, who sword in hand
Has devastated many a land
    And strewed his path with ghastly death!

II.

"How numerous are your destined prey
Adjudged to death beneath your sway?"
The traveler said. The Plague's reply,
"Three thousand citizens shall die!"
    Sank to his heart a poisoned dart.

III.

In time the travelers met again.
"You threatened three and murdered ten!"
Declared the man. The Plague replied:
"I killed but three; the rest that died
    If known aright, were killed by fright."

THE VISION OF A SPECTER.

I.

I FELL into a languid swoon
And slumbered at the height of noon;
And in my slumber plainly heard
A voice with half prophetic word,
As if proceeding from my side,
Shriek loudly, "Rise and view thy bride!"

II.

Half startled at the hideous sound,
I woke, arose and gazed around;
But when I saw no visible face
Of either living form or dead,
Thought I, "'Tis but a lingering trace
Of some faint vision of the head!"
With this I reassumed my place
Of rest upon the matted bed,
And pondering the vision deep,
Precipitately fell asleep;
And ere the echoes hardly died,
It shrieked again, "Behold thy bride!

III.

Weary at length—who would deny?—
Of this monotonous, hideous cry,
I sternly said ere half awake—
"Depart my room for Mercy's sake!
Why came you here to mar my rest?"
At this the Specter neared my side,
And with his hideous voice replied—
"Thou shouldst not thus be over weary!
For Time in time will bring the tide
Of hopeless years and visions dreary!
This time for thee—alas!—too soon,
Who slumbereth thus at height of noon!
But to my dreadful task I must
So arm thyself to bear the worst!"

IV.

As spake this bold intruder rude,
My trembling heart was quite subdued ;
" This is," thought I, "the Angel of Death !"
But soon to ease my heart occurred
To me the tenor of his word ;
" For me not death," I cried, " but life !
But oh ! what hath befallen my wife,
That thou shouldst through my window stride,
And bid me thus behold my bride ?"
At this the Specter waved his wand,
And bade me in his presence stand !
With terror dumb and wild dismay,
Trembling. I ventured to obey ;
The Specter waved aloft his wand,
And tapped me gently with his hand,
And told me that he came no foe ;
" But hark !" said he, " I've come to show
Thy youthful mind what shall befall
Thyself, thy wife, thy friends, thy all !"

V.

At this I courage took to hear
Whatever tale he chose to tell ;
His voice was smoother now and clear,
Foretokening still that all was well ;
But when he started his discourse,
I found his theme to be a curse !
" Thou'rt in the prime of youth," said he ;
" Thy heart is blithesome, buoyant, free ;
But thou—alas !—hast gone astray !
Therefore, henceforward from to day,
Shall be for thee no joy no peace,
Till worn by time and care shall cease
Thy sorrowful heart to palpitate,
Thy laboring soul to strive and wait !"
Then seizing me he bade me look
Into his everlasting book :
I looked ; and lo ! upon the sheet
I saw my photograph complete !
I gazed with terror and surprise ;
I then disputed with my eyes ;
But finding on the sheet a square
Of writing legible and fair,

I thither bent my wondering gaze
And read with terror and amaze—
" Behold emerging out of youth,
A temple built for Love and Truth !
How like a God erect he stands !
How like a school-girl's are his hands !
His opening mind, how heavily fraught
With love, and joy and every thought——"
Whatever else was written there
The Specter may himself declare ;
For here he snatched from me the book,
And with a proud, disdainful look,
Began to turn the pages o'er
In quest of what is yet in store.

VI.

And as he turned the pages by
I saw whole generations die !
And heard, or seemed to hear, the cries
That are to rend the eternal skies !
Hearing at length a joyous shout,
And seeing the flames dart fiercely out,
I slapped my hand upon the page
Where joy was mingled thus with rage,
And asked the Specter if I might
A moment gaze upon the sight.
"These fools ?" said he ; " for such they are
Who slay each other thus in war !"
I saw the hostile banners rise ;
I heard the whoop that tore the skies ;
And when their leaders gave command,
The strength and pride of many a land
Together rushed and fought and bled
As if from Earth had reason fled !
And when I heard the cannon's roar,
I quit the scene, and said, " No more
Of war for me !"   The ghost replied—
"These wars are all in store for earth !
And if thy valor ne'er is tried,
Thou well mayst praise thy peaceful birth ;
For as the ages roll along,
War gathers home her valiant throng !"

VII.

With this the Specter seized the book,
And said by my consent he'd look
The records o'er of War and Fame, ·
And tell me when he found my name.
He turned the pages one by one
From where man's history first begun ;
I looked thereon.   I saw disease
In forms too dread and foul to name ;
I saw mankind as by degrees
They changed till they were not the same
In shape or look ; and last of all
I saw my own unwelcome pall !
But war or peace I could not tell,
For prostrate on the floor I fell ;
The Specter waved aloft his wand,
And gave me power to rise and stand ;
But when he gave me back the book,
My hand so violently shook,
That on the floor with hideous roar
This direful roll of sorrows fell,
Complete of ours and those in Hell !
The Specter then with scornful look,
Commanded me to gaze the book !
With heavy soul and straining eyes
I viewed that book of monstrous size ;
For on the back in wondrous plan
The letters of the title ran—
I read, and lo! THE DOOM OF MAN!

VIII.

I turned to view the Specter's face,
But it had vanished into space !
I turned again to view the book,
But it had vanished out of sight !
Specter and all had ta'en its flight !
The Specter's vision now had fled ;
And I was lying on the bed
With heavy heart and aching head.

THE MONSTER.

I.

THE sun was set. And as the last
Glimmer of light was fading fast,
A monster p-rched upon the sands
        Where Cairo stands!

II.

A monster hideous as the Plague—
And shook his ulcerous arm and leg,
And swore to slay at one fell stroke
        'One half the folk!

III.

The frightened citizens knew not
How to escape the curse of what
Each in his fancy deemed a god
        As forth he strode.

IV.

'Twas plain he was a deity
Stained with the blood of victory
Gain-d in some fight above the clouds.
        Among the gods!

V.

Some built an altar-place and slew
The sacrifice; and though they knew
Not e'en the name the monster bore,
        Sought to adore!

IV.

Thus these in utter depths of night
Paid homage; every living wight
Trembling with mute astonishment
        And gaze intent!

VII.

The monster though he felt the power
To smite the throng and in an hour
To desolate the land, still knew
        What best to do.

VIII.

His power he held while he would smite
Both man and cattle; his delight
Was first to smite the beast and then
    To slay the men.

IX.

He knew if man into his arm
Would graft the virus that his harm
Was o'er; therefore the cattle he
    Smote cautiously.

X.

There stood a cow near by; he felt
All lenient as the stroke he dealt
To her—but e'en to draw his breath
    Was certain death!

XI.

The throng beheld with wild surprise;
And gazing on the darkening skies,
Piled sacrifice to this new lord
    Adored—abhorred!

XII.

The monster then somewhat at ease,
Let loose the power of his disease;
And thousands with the ulcerous wound
    Lay dead around!

XIII.

In later times in bloody raid
He slew more mortals than the blade;
Where'er he went he filled the tomb
    And scattered gloom!

XIV.

But his like every other's time
Wound to a close; inured to crime,
He careless grew and 'gan to make
    A foul mistake:

XV.

It bred such joy to deal the stroke
That o'er his ancient rule he broke
And slew by thousands man and beast
    Throughout the East.

XVI.

In one of his excursions he
Found man had stolen his victory;
The bovine virus had been tried
   And him defied!

XVII.

And now man holds within his hands
The power to banish from these lands
This ancient pest—yet strange to say,
   We still delay.

———:o:———

THE ARRIVAL.

I.

WINDS were raging on the sea,
  Heaving wildly with commotion;
Shallow vessels boisterously
  Tumbled o'er the hungry ocean:
Day by day the anxious crowds
  Sought a glimmer of the vision
Of the waving of the shrouds
  Scorning tempest with Elysian.

II.

All aboard was black despair,
  Grief and agonizing terror;
Maidens—raving—tore their hair;
  Tars—carousing—cursed their error:
Still upon the silent beach
  Stood in anxious expectation
Parents, friends and lovers—each
  Anxious for the crew's salvation.

III.

"Work, you jolly tar!" resounds
  Far across the chafing ocean;
"Sprung another leak!" confounds
  Every sense with wild commotion!

O how little know their friends
  Far beyond the angry waters
Of the woe that hovers round
  Parents, lovers, sons and daughters!

IV.

Ah! a glimmer breaks the spell!
  Haven breaks upon the vision!
Shout ye tars that now can tell
  Scorn to tempest in derision!
"Ha! They're safe!" resounds afar
  From the gaz-rs oy the ocean;
"Safe and rescued from the proud
  Tempest raving in its motion!"

V.

Hope inspires the weary breast;
  Joy succeeds to lamentation;
Winds have ceased—the billows rest
  Calmly on the sea's foundation!
All is mingled joy and glee;
  Signs exchange with signs;—the vision
Half portrays but silently
  Winds o'erthrown and in derision!

VI.

Joy is high! The opening port
  Trembles with the vessel's motion;—
Down she goes with bubbling sound
  To the yawning caves of ocean!
O what horrors seize upon
  Parent, husband, sister, brother,
Wife and daughter, lover—*all!*
  Hope's a fiend! Despair's another!

IN THE WOODS.

I.

WHAT a nameless feeling it instills
To wander through the pathless woods alone,
To hear the music of the rippling rills
That plunge along upon their beds of stone!
How sweet to view the scenery on the hills
Our feet ascended in the days agone!
We pause to think; and vainly wish to be
In childhood once again so pure and free.

II.

But this cannot; once launched upon the sea
Of Time we learn (and oh, how oft too late!)
That we are ushered on and on till we
Have but a dim remembrance of the state
We first enjoyed; the primal purity
Of life is gone; and yielding to our fate,
We see tempestuous clouds but dare not shrink
Although we stand on foul Destruction's brink!

III.

I know there are who claim that "man is free,"
And of his mis-ries make a lengthy text
To prove that all things are as they should be—
Reflected down to *this* world from the *next*;
I know there are who cannot bear to see
A weary wight with inmost soul perplexed;
This well I know—but can't suppress the strain
That tells of woe and labor spent in vain.

IV.

The noise of Pomp allures us to its fane;
We catch a glimpse and henceforth are but slaves;
Ambition scatters round his fatal bane
That poisons Purity and all that craves
A holier life; and Science lures the brain,
And builds a temple darker than the graves;
And all combine to make the man of Earth
Curse his nativity and rue his birth.

V.

Thus life amid the strife and jarring throng ;
How different far when in the silent wood
Where every breeze that passes soft along
Inspires the heart and gives the spirit food !
'Tis here we listen to the ancient song
That Nature sang of old when unsubdued,
We climbed the hills and with our infant eyes
Peered through the foliage to the bending skies.

VI.

To pay these earlier haunts a passing stroll
Inspires with raptures all the inner man ;
The spirits of Poetry and of Silence roll
Their airy flight around ; and all that can
In any way absorb the thinking soul
Loom up around till we adore the plan
Of Nature, though perchance a "broken heart"
Forbids us to enjoy the tastes of Art.

————:o:————

THE LOSS OF YOUTH.

I.

VISIONS of the lovely Day!
  Ye half inspire me with delight !
As far as gleams the visual ray
  Fresh Nature blooms and shakes in light ;
The crystal brook flows on serene
The verdurous, rounded hills between ;
The songsters of the air resound
The beauties of the scene around.

II.

Yet I am sad !   And what the cause ?
  A love for times I can't forget ;
I mourn—'tis one of Nature's laws—
  The sun of Youth forever set !
'Tis vain to retrospect through time
To prove that sorrow springs from crime ;
I mourn—dispute the fact who can ?--
That I've at last become a man !

The Midnight Soliloquy.

I.

ALONE I sit! 'Twas midnight long ago;
And all but me ere now have gone to rest:—
The babe lies sleeping on its mother's breast,
The happiest thing on this Terrene below;

II.

The school-boy laid his books and papers by
Three hours ago, and closed his eyes for sleep;
All mourners now but me have ceased to weep,
And wipe the tear-drop from the watery eye;

III.

Both great and poor—besides myself—it seems
Have dropped their cares to spend in rest the night;
But I am doomed to sit (O, horrid sight!)
To sit alone debarred of rest and dreams!

IV.

And what the cause? A restless state of mind:
A doubtful fear of—who can tell me what?
A thirst for that which is and yet is not;
A dread of what o'erhangs all human kind!

V.

A love for what I ne'er expect to see;
A doubt of what were else my blessings here;
A sorrow that survives in many a tear;
A hope—alas! what hope remains for me!

VI.

Still here I sit! Before me Darkness reigns;
Behind me naught but weakness can be found;
A forlorn, wretched cumberer of the ground!
My life a glimpse—then who knows what remains?

VII.

'Tis thus when man his course of life reviews:
What else were his, of slight account he deems
And spurns aside; and lives inwrapped in dreams
Of future hopes and fears, a vain recluse.

VIII.

Could childhood wrap my feeble senses in,
Nor let them stray their lonely circuit round,
No bliss like mine could anywhere be found;—
Alas for those who know the paths of sin!

IX.

Still here I sit—unknown to sleep and rest—
Desiring all and yet receiving none!
Thus many a night till rises forth the Sun
And shoots his sparkling beams throughout the West.

X.

And what reward awaits me when I'm done?
Alas! who knows the state beneath the sod
Where man returns in silence to his God,
A withered worm whose earthly race is run!

XI.

Alas! we can but know his Earthly store:
Desire and hope and dread and want and fear,
His constant goods; and when his hopes are clear,
Out goes his light—and he is known no more!

———:o:———

A FRAGMENT.

WHEN on Mount Libanus of ancient fame
    The old man of the Mountain marshalled forth
His gloomy devotees for deeds of shame
    And sent them roving up and down the Earth
Bent on their prey like Satan when he came
    'Gainst honest Job, no potentate of Earth
Could for a moment deem himself secure,
So daring were the fiends and so impure.

THE TOMB OF HOPE.

I.

THE voice of the Past
As it rides on the blast
Is a dirge to the Soul with woes overcast;
And for the Hope he reveres
As the staff of his years
But a dark-gleaming tomb stone is all that appears!

II.

When the sunshine of Youth
And the pure love of Truth
Could wrest the live honey from Care's poison tooth—
Full little he then
Knew the tortures of men
When the dark tomb of Hope casts its shade on the glen!

III.

But he still ushered on,
And on and still on,
Till the season of Youth and its pleasures were gone;
And he now stands before
The dark tomb and reads o'er
The burden of Hope's epitaph—" Nevermore !"

IV.

'Tis done ;—and the woe
Of the dark Long Ago
Now beats on the Soul with a withering blow;
And the visions of yore
Are all blasted before
The burden of Hope's epitaph--" NEVERMORE !"

PART EIGHTH.

THE FATHER'S FAREWELL.

I.

ADIEU, thou disobedient son!
  Oft have I striven but in vain
To check the course that thou hast run,
  And freely poured my tears as rain!
With thee I've spent the wakeful night;
With thee I've shared thy far delight;
For thee I've felt the reuding pain;
For thee I've labored long in vain!

II.

And now farewell!   I would not do
  To thee as thou hast done to me;
I would not pierce thy spirit through
  And make a boast of Victory.
Thou hast my warmest blessings spurned;
From my advices thou hast turned;
Thou hast rejected Love and Truth,
And followed phantasies of Youth!

THE MISER.

I.

THE wind blew shrill. The miser crept
From out his dark and dusty room—
More aptly called a living tomb—
Wherein he lay but never slept;
And now in deepest depth of night,
Without the semblance of a light,
He seeks his gold so long his bane
And clasps it to his heart again!

II.

O depth of Misery and Night!
   The miser bending o'er his gold
   With bony hand and heart as cold
As Polar ice, disdains the sight
Of Love and Joy and Happiness,
And buys with gold his deep distress!
If this were money's purest end
Well might we change its name to "*Fiend!*"

III.

'Tis thus the miser spends his time:
   The winds around his cabin door
   Still chant his mournful dirges o'er,
As deep and deeper sinks in crime
The slave of gold, the skeleton fool
Whose life-blood now begins to cool;
Erelong upon his bed of rags
He falls—and dies among his bags!

IV.

The miser takes his leap for aye
   ʼFrom earth; and as we hear his knell
   With deep regret the tale we tell
Of how his soul was borne away;
Then comes a feeling of relief
That checks the rising sigh of grief:
" He's gone to dwell beneath the tomb,
That better men may have his room !"

THE SILENT BEGGAR.

I.

THE voice of Music and the voice of Love
Re echoed sweetly through the palace hall
And woke the echoes of supreme delight:
    A beggar stood a pondering how to prove
    His wretchedness and yet not to appall
    The joyous inmates sheltered from the night!

II.

Inside the hall 'tis happiness supreme;
Love sweetens every tone that freights the air
And brilliancy adorns the sweet delight:
    Without 'tis as a fever-haunted dream;
    The wailing winds are echoes of despair
    And ushers of the miseries of night!

III.

Inside the palace Love begins to hold
His revels in the maiden lap of Youth
And fill his devotees with sweet delight:
    The wind arises heavier and cold;
    The beggar sighs aloud the fatal truth—
    " Age cannot long withstand this gusty night!"

IV.

The voice of lovers in their locked embrace
Is heard within the ancient palace hall
Where maidens tremble at the nuptial vow—
    But oh! what agonies and woe I trace
    On his decrepit brow whose opening pall
    Disturbs the troubled vision even now!

V.

'Tis sweetness all and fathomless delight
Around the festal boards where voice of Love
Re-echoes bick to Love that speaks again:
    The ancient beggar shivering in the night
    Would rather die of hunger than to prove
    A recreant among the sons of men!

VI.

Full many a lad and many a lovely lass
Account their sorrows murdered with delight
Since their arrival at the beauteous dome:
    The ancient beggar struck his cane to pass
    Ahead into the gusty realm of night,
    Awed by remembrance of his ancient home!

VII.

The voice of Music still resounds within;
Still heave the youthful hearts with sweet delight
As touched with the celestial lamp of Joy:
    Again the ancient beggar did begin
    To seek his journey through the darksome night
    That threatened all his vigor to destroy!

VIII.

The dead of night has stolen upon the scene;
The gayeties are winding to a close
That solace furnished for so many a wight:
    The crowds disperse; when lo! with frightful mien
    A ragged beggar—heir to countless woes—
    O'erthrown and slain by the inclement night!

————:o:————

THE SMILES.

I.

THE Earth was robed with glistening snow;
    The sun had long forborne his rays;
The clouds hung heavy, dull and low,
    Fraught with the *gloom* of wintry days;—
        When burst a gleam of solar light
        That smiles inspired of pure delight.

II.

A youth whose pleasure was to roam
    Had strayed o'er many a distant plain
When memories of his lovely home
    Induced him to return again;
        The sire to meet the wanderer went
        And smiles exchanged of pure content.

III.

Two lovers by the parlor fire
  In secret clasp enjoy their rest ;
" Art mine ?"   " Thou know'st 'tis my desire !"
  Of burden frees each throbbing breast ;
    And, as the traitorous blushes prove,
    Each face is fraught with smiles of love.

————:o:————

BENJAMIN STRATT.

BENJAMIN STRATT was a bachelor old
  Who seemed to live but for his gold ;
By toil incessant, spurning rest,
He gained the Mount of Fortune's crest ;
But what true joy can spring from gold ?—
The miser's heart is always cold.
'Tis said that Ben when in his youth
Had loftier views of Love and Truth,
And that his earlier love was spurned ;
He then shut up his heart and turned
His thoughts toward money—and in time,
By toil incessant and by crime,
Accumulated wealth till he
The richest man was said to be
In all the land.   He then began
To think of love and how to scan
The distance measureless between
Himself and her whose face serene
Inspired his inmost soul with fire ;
At length he roused and struck the lyre :
" 'Tis long since I have thought of love,
But now its power revives again,
As all my trembling system proves !
Wilt thou depart from single life,
And joined in love become my wife ?"
" What wouldst thou do ?" quoth she amain,
" To prove thy love ?"   Poor Ben turned pale,
And trembling offered to curtail

His daily rations; and to bring
His heart an humble offering.
" And wilt thou clothe the poor?" she cried.
" I will—if thou wilt be my bride!"
" Wilt thou give alms to those that preach
The Sacred Word within thy reach?"
Ben turning pale made promise due
And trembling asked what else to do.
"Wilt thou refit thy house?" Ben said
He'd lived therein for thirty years,
And that the furniture though worn
Was good enough. His love replied:
" If thou wouldst have me for thy bride
Refit thy rooms; 'twill cost at most
Not one per cent of what thou hast."
Ben faltered—stammered—then replied,
" I will—if thou wilt be my bride!"
" Wilt thou forget thy gold the while
And dress in fashionable style?"
Here Benny failed; he could not spend
His gold for such a worthless end;
But offered still to dress the while
His wife in fashionable style!
She rose—somewhat at liberty—
And said, "Thou art too cold for me!
The man that for his lover's sake
Cannot the miser's habits break
Need not invite me for his wife—
I'd much prefer a single life!"

PART NINTH.

To the Pyramid of Cheops.

I.

CHEOPS, what art thou? tomb;
Column for him to view who round thee plods;
Or ruined temple where the flush and bloom
    Of youth adored the Gods?

II.

How long hast thou withstood
The rolling storms that bellow round thy throne?
Wilt thou not tell? or hast not understood
    How swiftly Time hath flown?

III.

Who reared thy crest in air?
Speak—for the anxious world awaits to hear.
Have kings dwelt round thy throne that they might stare
    On thee from year to year?

IV.

Since first thy lofty crest
Flashed in the sunlight glistening from afar,
The world hath greatly changed, but had no rest
From loud and cruel war.

V.

Hast thou not quaked with fear,
When hostile armies hailed from lands unknown,
And with the saber, cannon, club and spear,
Fought battles round thy throne?

VI.

When steel-clad armies shook
The Eastern World, and rushed without a check
O'er stately thrones—didst thou in silence look
Upon the fearful wreck?

VII.

Since thou wast throned of yore,
The Grecian, Persian, Roman, Arab, Turk,
Yea, Frank and Saxon, all have fought before
Thy face 'mid storm and murk!

VIII.

Earth's mightiest monarchies
Have risen and reigned and fallen before thy face,
And left the record of their dynasties
In many a warlike trace;

IX.

And Science hath unfurled
Her balmy wing, and ta'en her distant flight
Into the West, leaving the Eastern World
To Barbarism and Night;

X.

Yet still thou rearest thy head
From off the ruins of thine ancient land
From which all culture, power and light have fled—
All but the ruins and sand.

JERUSALEM.

I.

JERUSALEM! how thy name awakes the soul
Of him who knows thy state in ages past,
Since on thy hills the Jews assembled last,
To praise Jehovah, refuge from Sheol!

II.

Though stranger kings have leveled with the ground
Thy walls, and torn thy holy Temple down,
That on thy name shed luster and renown
A thousand years through all the regions round—

III.

Though stranger gods o'er thee have held their sway
And reaped the praises due to Israel's God—
Though Pagans, Christians, Islams, all have trod
Thy sacred streets and hastened their decay—

IV.

Thou'rt yet and still shalt be the Jew's delight,
Who hold as naught all earthly praise but thine,
And still expect upon thy hills to shine
Messiah's face at breaking up of Night!

V.

Nor is thy name less sacred held by those
Whose every act delares themselves to be
Determined foes to Israel and to thee;
How complicate the tenets of thy foes!

VI.

Since from thy sacred hills triumphant shone
Great Cæsar's blood stained banner waving high,
Undecked has been thy face, unheard thy cry,
And thou hast been by alien powers cast down.

VII.

The Roman, Persian, Arab, Osman, all
Have turn by turn despoiled thy sacred lands;
And e'en crusaders with their blood stained hands
Have swayed thy scepter—finished up thy fall!

VIII.

Meanwhile thy guardian race afar dispersed
By tyrants were forbid to see thy face;
Thus eighteen centuries; yet time nor place
Has changed the dogmas by their sires rehearsed!

IX.

And though Destruction has defaced thy mount
Till naught of former grandeur now remains,
Thy sons still hope to break their servile chains,
Rebuild thy glory, drink from out thy fount!

X.

Just God! why lies Thy ancient city thus?
Why rules the Moslem o'er Thy chosen land?
Why not the Jew permitted be to stand
Upon these hills so famed in ancient verse?

XI.

Is not Thy cup of vengeance emptied yet?
Shall Israel's days of sorrow have no end?
Shall Judah's sons no more thy hills ascend
And offer praises where their freedom set?

XII.

Yes! Time will roll till fair Jerusalem
Shall reascend from out her worn debris,
Resume her station, prove herself to be
The Jews' inheritance—their priceless gem!

————:o:————

THE CRUSADERS AT JERUSALEM.

I.

JERUSALEM swims in blood! anon
  The dread commanders spend new breath
To urge their fiery warriors on
      To deeds of Death.

II.

The sacred hills where in the days
Of yore full many a worthy trod,
Are filled with slaughter for the praise
    Of Judah's God!

III.

Fanaticism inspires the hearts
Of armies hailing from afar,
And all the power to vigor starts
    That dwells in war.

IV.

The inhuman sound of woman's cry
Dies off, nor on the 'warrior's ear
Makes noted impress; lowers the sky
    Dark, bleak and drear.

V.

The thunders of Almighty Power
Are rolling o'er the destined throng;
And in an unprepared hour
    Sweep all along.

VI.

Dire sounds the war, and dire the cry
Ascends from the tumultuous crowd;
While sulphurous smoke ascending high
    .   Forms quite a cloud.

VII.

Jerusalem on her ancient hills
Ne'er felt but once a bloodier war;
But this the prophecy fulfills
    Of times afar.

VIII.

Behold! where Solomon's Temple stood,
A citadel with blood is drenched!   _
Crusaders' thirst for tears and blood
    Cannot be quenched.

IX.

A mob at least ten thousand strong
Are murdered, and the horrid cry
Ascends amid the conqueror's song
    The crimson sky.

X.

And now behold! with dripping hands
The dread Crusaders kneel before
The Sepulcher; these murdering bands
    Their God adore!

XI.

O depths of Infamy and Shame!
Let reason pluck the life of War;
And Justice tremble at the name,
    And stand afar.

XII.

'Tis o'er; Jerusalem, piled on heaps,
Sends forth an agonizing groan;
And Godefroy aided by the Powers
    Ascends the throne.

XIV.

And while tumultuous clouds surround
Of wars and tears, he sits secure
On Salem's throne; a sovereign crowned
    With heart impure.

XV.

Thus Judah, Fate decreed thy doom,
Since thou didst scorn thy rightful Lord;
Thy fall begun when crushed by Rome,
    And ends abhorred.

XVI.

Yet thou wilt rear thy head on high
When better times thy power release,
And hail beneath a gracious sky,
    Returning Peace!

Moscow.

I.

ABANDONED to a furious foe
    Whose code of war all nations know,
Thou art adjudged to scenes of woe,
                Moscow!

II.

The greatest warrior earth hath known,
Surveys thee—powerless and alone—
And deems thy palaces his own,
                Moscow!

III.

Then rouse thee to thy double might!
Pass round the cheers and enter fight;
The earth shall judge who's in the right,
                Moscow!

IV.

Thou art the key to Fortune's door,
Than which Napoleon asks no more;
Defeated here his game is o'er,
                Moscow!

V.

Ha! whence those flames that wrap the sky?
Hast thou resolved for once to try
A suicidal victory?
                Moscow!

VI.

'Tis o'er; the invader now must flee;
One struggle more and earth is free!
Whom should we honor more than thee?
                Moscow!

THE BATTLE OF TRAFALGAR.

I.

THE battle stood. The frightened whale
  Sunk to the caverns of the sea;
The birds ascended; then the gale
    Burst wild and free.

II.

The Saxon and the Frank have met
  Once more in battle; tears and blood
Are freely poured upon the jet
    And startled flood.

III.

From many a brazen gun the flame
  Burst fiercely forth—a vivid stream—
And nations trembled at the name
    That's now our theme.

IV.

Dread lightnings flashed from shore to shore;
  Infernal thunders shook the world;
And France and Albion rushed through gore
    With flag unfurled.

V.

Cadiz, from off her island throne,
  Gazed seaward; trembled at the roar,
Gibraltar on his heaps of stone
    And marred his shore.

VI.

Great was the loss and great the woe
  That this king-making battle cost;
'Tis o'er; and e'en the victory
    To us is lost.

VII.

The fight is lost to all but Fame;
  Dread Fame that stands amid the war,
And shouts in thunder tones the name
    Of "Trafalgar!"

CADIZ.

I.

ERE Rome's foundation stone
Was hewn or placed, or London had her birth,
Or dynasty assumed a royal throne
  That figures on the Earth;

II.

Ere Grecian heroes trod
The fields of Glory or the assembled throngs
Beneath the Temple's roof adored their God
  In prayer and fervent songs;

III:

While round the Earth was thrown—
One Land except—a darkness deep, profound;—
Cadiz from off her sea-bound island shone
  Conspicuous far around.

IV.

For thrice a thousand years,
'Mid wreck of falling empires and the groan,
Or armed with roaring guns or armed with spears,
  Her isle has been her throne.

V.

As ages rolled along,
The native Celt, the Roman, Goth and Moor,
Each in his turn with sinewy arm and strong
  Spread tumult round her shore.

VI.

Full many a Pagan breathed
From in her bounds his spirit back to God;
Yea, Islam too; since when in glory wreathed
  Her shores have Christians trod.

VII.

Should cycles endless roll
O'er Earth as now 'tis formed, her active part
Of countless scenes from out the human soul
  Would never, ne'er depart.

THE TURK-BELL.

I.

"CONSTANTINOPLE powerless stands
A powerful city!" cried the Turk;
And marshalled forth his valiant bands,
    And set to work.

II.

The East already owned his sway;
His pride was at Ambition's height;
His valor feared no fight by day
    Nor plot by night.

III.

Around him gathered at his call
His war-chiefs filled with zeal for war,
And swore to conquer or to fall
    In climes afar.

IV.

The Islam horde with flag unfurled
To conquest marched beyond the Strait,
And filled with fury bade the world
    Yield to her fate.

V.

And Europe—O, what deep disgrace!—
Filled with intestine violence,
Stood mute and in the " Turk bell " placed
    Her confidence !

VI.

Brief was the war.   The Sultan gained
Constantinople's barracks; and
His dynasty has since profaned
    The Grecian land.

VII.

Let States no more a barbarous horde
Strive to impede with Heavenly arms;
Or ring the " Turk-bell " when the cloud
    Of war alarms !

THE FAME OF JERUSALEM.

I.

JERUSALEM! thou City of God,
  Wherein the wise king Solomon trod!
Why hast thou been in later time
    The seat of Crime?

II.

Thy day of power is gone;
When Rome sat foot upon
Thy sacred hills, she hurl'd the blight
    Of deepest Night!

III.

Proudest of ancient cities, thou
Hast outlived War; and even now
Though trampled by the foe, thy name
    Still shines the same.

IV.

Imperial Rome would sooner fail
To lure the traveler, or the wail
Of Babylon cease to rend the sky,
    Than thou wouldst die.

V.

Thou judgment-place of Jesus!   Who
Can give thy name the reverence due?
When we remember whither trod
    The Son of God!

VI.

O'er every place beneath the sky
Hang dark Oblivion's curtains high;
But thou hast plucked 'mid scenes of strife
    The Tree of Life!

www.ingramcontent.com/pod-product-compliance
Lightning Source LLC
Chambersburg PA
CBHW021122020726

47500CB00003B/876